SAKEV

CONQUERED WORLD: BOOK FOUR

ELIN WYN

CLOCK
WALK
PUBLISHING

SAKEV

"Is it too much to ask for one of these trees to come to life?" I looked from mossy trunk to mossy trunk for some sign of movement.

"Why would you want that in the first place?" Axtin, our resident heavy hitter, replied.

I'd think he'd be the first to jump at the chance to fight one of the sentient tree beasts that roamed the forest.

"Because as much as I love our daily nature walks," I started, practically feeling Vrehx bristle at my description of our routine patrols, "I'd like to do something useful."

"How is fighting one of those skrell walking trees useful?" Vrehx asked.

I'd gotten under his skin. It was an art form I'd

perfected by this time. One day, it was going to get me punched in the face, but it wouldn't be the first time.

"Maybe it's not useful, but it's entertaining." I grinned back.

"So, you're whining because you're bored?" Vrehx sighed. "Sorry the Xathi war isn't *entertaining* enough."

"Don't get me wrong. Fighting the Xathi, saving people, and all that good stuff are plenty entertaining. We just don't do any of that very often," I remarked. "You can't expect me to believe that the best we can do is to walk along the same forest paths every day."

Alright. It wasn't the same paths over and over. That would be stupid. But we'd covered so much of the surrounding area it all looked the same.

Aside from a few isolated incidents, we'd barely made a dent against the Xathi invasion. The massive, crystalline, insect-like creatures had been slowly choking the life out of this planet. The humans who inhabited it were ill-prepared for something like this.

When we'd fallen through the rift in space and landed here, we became their only hope. And the best we could do was stroll through the woods near our ship, the *Vengeance*.

It wasn't enough, but it looked like I was the only one who'd admit it.

"Do you want to be on galley duty tonight? If so, keep running your mouth," Vrehx seethed.

I was having fun now. The others in our strike team were silent, but I could see by the tightness in the corners of their mouths and the rigid way they held their shoulders that they were trying not to laugh.

"I don't mind helping out in the galley. Snipes is a good guy, though his cooking leaves much to be desired." I shrugged.

Axtin snorted.

"Silence," Tu'ver said sharply. He'd stopped moving entirely.

The witty remark I'd planned died in my throat.

I gave Tu'ver as hard of a time as I gave everyone else, but when he stood still like that in the field, even I knew it was best to shut my trap.

"What is it?" Vrehx asked in a hushed voice.

"Movement to the east. Whatever it is, there's more than one." Tu'ver lifted his impressive rifle and peered through the scope. I knew it had a ton of fancy upgrades and mods, not that Tu'ver would ever let me try it out.

"There's a refugee camp somewhere nearby," Axtin said. "Maybe it's them."

"Let's check it out," Vrehx ordered. "We'll offer aid if we can. Is that a satisfactory use of your time, Sakev?"

"It's not taking down a sentient tree, but I guess it'll do." I grinned.

If there were people nearby, fleeing the Xathi, of

course I wanted to help them. Since we were no closer
to actually defeating the Xathi, helping people was the
next best thing.

"I'm going to get a better vantage point." Tu'ver
quickly scaled a tree and disappeared into the canopy.

It's hard to believe someone that big could move like
that. K'vers weren't as heavily built as Skotans, but
Tu'ver and I were of similar heights and builds.

I definitely outweighed him, though. A branch that
supported him would snap under me.

It wasn't long before Tu'ver's voice crackled through
our radios.

"Not humans. Hybrids. Four of them. Hunting for
something."

"Didn't you say there were refugees in the area?" I
asked Vrehx, who nodded. "That must be what they're
hunting. We have to take the hybrids out."

Tu'ver dropped out of the tree and landed silently
beside Vrehx. Under different circumstances, I
would've been equally impressed and creeped out. He
moved way too quietly.

"Do we have a location on the human refugees?"
Vrehx asked.

"They move each day," Tu'ver replied. "They weren't
far from here yesterday, but who knows where they are
now."

"What does it matter?" I asked. "The hybrids will

find them eventually, no matter where they are. We have to take them down."

"We don't know that the hybrids are hunting the refugees," Vrehx replied.

"What else would they be hunting?" Axtin asked.

"Us," was Tu'ver's grim reply. "It must be driving the Queen mad knowing we're here but being unable to find us."

The *Vengeance* had the most sophisticated cloaking device I'd ever seen. I didn't fully understand how it worked, but it was extremely effective. We'd been here for quite a while, and the Xathi still didn't know where we were.

"Is that less of a reason to grind them into dust?" I asked, though I was largely ignored.

I guess that's what I got for pissing Vrehx off. Fair enough.

While the others went back and forth about the best course of action, I pulled a small gadget out of my pack. It was something I'd been working on to beat the boredom of stagnant ship life.

It was a standard scanner that measured heat signatures, but I'd amped it up. It could scan farther and in more detail.

In theory, at least.

I'd never actually tested it.

I quietly powered it up and scanned the

surrounding forest. The good news was, it worked like a charm. Heat signatures lit up the tiny screen, mostly small creatures of the forest.

There was a large clump moving strangely. That had to be the hybrids.

To the south, much closer than I would have liked, was another large group. The refugees.

The hybrids were moving towards them quickly, but before I could tell the others, the device threw sparks and the screen went black. It was totally fried.

My mind was racing. By the time Vrehx and the others decided on a course of action, it would be too late. They'd never believe what I saw, now that my scanner was busted.

It was only four hybrids, according to Tu'ver. They would be nothing but warm-up exercise.

I could get there, take them out, and get back in no time. The refugees would be safe, and my strike team wouldn't be at risk.

That would be a win-win scenario.

"I'll handle it," I said over my shoulder as I took off into the forest.

"Sakev, get back here! That's an order!" Vrehx yelled, but I wasn't going to stop now.

The hybrids were not stealthy movers. I heard them long before I saw them.

The first one never saw me coming as I fired a shot

through its skull. The other three wailed and hissed, throwing themselves at me.

As we fought, I noticed how they clicked and chirped to one other. Their attacks were more coordinated than they had been the last time I fought them.

It was unusual for the Xathi to create slaves with any level of intelligence or autonomy. It was definitely worth mentioning to Rouhr.

I felled a second one. This would be over in no time.

I was already planning how I was going to rub this in Vrehx's face. It'd probably earn me galley duty for a month, but it'd be worth it. And I really did like hanging out with Snipes.

One of the hybrids paused long enough to let out an ear-shattering screech. I'd heard it before. It was calling for reinforcements.

There must've been other groups nearby, groups Tu'ver hadn't seen.

"You're going to get us all killed!" a voiced yelled from behind me. The rest of my strike team emerged from the trees to join the brawl.

"You weren't supposed to follow me!" I shouted back, but my words were drowned out by the sound of approaching hybrids.

Lots of them.

"Skrell!"

We were overwhelmed. They were everywhere, more than I could count.

"Call for an evac!" Tu'ver shouted over the chaos.

I barely heard Vrehx shouting into his radio. A hybrid scrambled toward me, but I didn't have enough time to react.

It practically exploded, just feet away from me, as Axtin's gigantic hammer smashed into its side. Shards of crystal flew everywhere. I howled as a thick shard embedded itself deep in my arm.

"Strike team two is coming," Vrehx called out. "We just need to hold out until then."

There was a gash on the side of his head. Blood trickled down his face, blending in with the red of his skin. Tu'ver was firing with his off hand, his good arm bent at an odd angle.

This was my fault.

We pulled together in a clump, firing and lashing out in any way we could.

The hybrids were smarter than they'd been before, but thankfully, most of them hadn't developed a thick crystal coating yet.

That was our only advantage.

One shot from a blaster would bring them down.

I heard the sound of a shuttle from somewhere above us. Strike team two descended on ropes, joining the fray with vigor. With our efforts and ammunitions doubled, we were eventually able to beat back the hybrids.

Those that didn't fall scurried back into the forest. No doubt the Xathi Queen already knew what transpired.

I looked around. No one had escaped unscathed, but we hadn't lost anyone, either.

This wasn't supposed to happen. I should've known they would follow me. It's a good thing they did, but they weren't supposed to get hurt.

The humans had a saying for this. I'd heard Axtin's human mate say it once or twice.

No good deed goes unpunished, or something like that.

Vrehx stood off to the side, talking into his radio. I walked up to him, but before I could open my mouth, he cut me off.

"Say even one word, and I will leave you here for the hybrids to pick apart."

I shut my mouth and nodded.

I deserved that.

EVIE

"Dr. Evie, I'm telling you! I'm sick to my stomach. I think I'm going to die!" The tiny voice came from the floor of my office.

I used the term "office" very loosely. In reality, it was just a small corner of the refugee bay, bordered by dingy curtains pulled together from who knows what or where.

I didn't mind, though. It was nice to have some semblance of normalcy.

I peered over the edge of my desk that doubled as an examination table. It was nothing more than a sheet of metal laid over two empty barrels.

One of my regular patients, a child named Calixta, was curled up on the floor, writhing in agony. It was a bit she played at least once a week, each time more dramatic and life threatening than the last.

By now, I suspected she knew she couldn't fool me, but she always tried. It was like a game, and I'd be lying if I said I didn't find it amusing. I looked forward to her visits.

"Calixta, if you're tummy is hurting as bad as you say it is, I might have to take out your appendix!"

Calixta peered up at me through a curtain of dark hair.

"That's fine," she said, completely straight-faced.

I couldn't help but laugh.

"What are you trying to avoid?" I walked around my desk to sit on the floor beside her.

I'd tried to liven the space up with a dusty old rug, but it didn't help much. I could still feel the cold of the metal floor seeping into me.

"Miss Vidia is teaching fractions, and I'm terrible at them," Calixta mumbled.

Vidia, the former mayor of Fraga, the city that I once called home, had taken it upon herself to continue the education of the children who now lived aboard the *Vengeance*. I couldn't think of anyone I admired more.

"You're always going to suck at fractions if you keep running away from them." I tucked a strand of hair away from her face.

I didn't know exactly what happened to Calixta's

parents, but they weren't here. Same for many of the other children that had made it to the *Vengeance*. We, the adults, all lent a hand in looking after them.

"Why do I even have to learn them? It's stupid." Calixta lifted her head from the floor and sat up.

"Leena had to learn fractions."

Leena was my ace in the hole when it came to Calixta. The renowned chemist all but adopted Calixta after they survived being captured by the Xathi.

"She did?" Calixta asked curiously.

"She sure did. And so did I. Leena couldn't be a chemist and I couldn't be a doctor if we didn't learn fractions."

Before Calixta could reply, the curtains of my office were pushed aside as a Skotan soldier entered.

I quickly glanced at Calixta to make sure she wasn't frightened.

The aliens rarely came into the human area. Some still felt uneasy around them, but Calixta didn't seem to mind. In fact, Calixta treated the aliens with more kindness and respect than most humans I knew.

"How can I help you?" I asked.

"General Rouhr requests your presence in the med bay at your earliest convenience."

I couldn't hide my surprise. General Rouhr ran things on the *Vengeance*, but I'd never met him. I didn't think he knew I existed.

"Calixta, please go to class." I gave the child an affectionate pat on the head. I helped her to her feet and ushered her into the main bay.

"And I'll be checking with Miss Vidia to make sure you attended!" I called after her as she ran off.

"Lead the way." I gestured to the soldier. He nodded.

As we made our way through the refugee bay, most of the people paid us no mind. Some stared, still not used to seeing aliens on a regular basis. Others outright sneered at us.

Even though we were alive because of the *Vengeance* crew, some people continued to hate aliens on principle. Those were the people I treated in my office. They refused the clearly superior care in the med bay simply because it wasn't human.

I didn't agree with their small-mindedness, but it gave me something to do.

I'd never been to the med bay, but I had to admit I was excited to see the sort of technology used for treatment. I heard it was run by a fully functioning AI that was decades ahead of the AI we'd developed on Ankau. I wondered if it was advanced enough for me to talk shop with.

"What does General Rouhr need me for?" I asked once we left the refugee bay.

"A strike team got into a scuffle out in the forest. Some hybrids got the better of them."

I'd heard talk of hybrids. They're horrible creatures, caught somewhere between human and Xathi. They're mindless slaves to the Xathi Queen.

Most of the humans were kept in the dark about what was happening outside the *Vengeance*. After what they'd been through, many preferred it that way.

Vidia often spoke with General Rouhr, offering knowledge of the towns. I got all of my information from her.

The med bay was a flurry of activity. Every bed was filled with soldiers in various injured states. One of them, a K'ver, definitely had a broken arm.

General Rouhr, a battle-worn Skotan, stood in the center with his fingers pressed into the bridge of his nose.

"You asked for me?" I approached cautiously.

"Evangeline Parr?" he asked, and I nodded. "Good. The med bay AI isn't performing to its full capabilities. We deactivated several functions to conserve power, since it wasn't being used. Ironically, now we need those functions. You have the most advanced medical training of anyone on board. I was hoping you'd be willing to pick up some of the slack until the AI is fully functional once more."

"Of course." I looked skeptically at the wounded soldiers. "But my training is for humans."

"How different can it be?" General Rouhr said with

a slight smile. It took me a moment to realize he was making a joke. "Your help is appreciated."

"Where should I start?"

I was anxious to work. Plus, this was a chance to learn more about the aliens I now lived alongside.

"Some of my crew has already started patching up the minor injuries," General Rouhr explained. "If it's all right with you, I'll have you start on our most severely wounded."

He pointed to a bed in the back of the med bay.

Another Skotan was twitching in pain, though clearly trying not to. His skin was more vibrant than General Rouhr's, likely indicating a younger age, though he was not lacking in scars.

"I'm on it." I hoped I didn't sound nervous.

The injured Skotan was huge. Well over six feet, if I had to guess, and very well built.

I almost didn't notice the thick crystal shard protruding from his arm. It looked like the spike went clean through the muscle. It must've been incredibly painful.

"Who let a human in here?" the Skotan said through a wince.

"General Rouhr asked me to assist with some injuries. I'm Dr. Evangeline Parr."

"Rouhr must want me dead if he's letting a human work on me," the Skotan hissed.

"My mortality rate is one of the lowest on the planet, so you needn't worry." I forced a tight smile onto my face. "Looks like someone met the business end of a hybrid."

"And here I was, thinking I just ate some bad stew," the Skotan snapped.

I didn't react. Pain made people lash out. I'd learned not to take rudeness personally.

I picked up the data pad mounted next to the bed and pulled up his medical information. Apparently, his name was Sakev.

I gasped at the sheer number of times he'd been admitted to the med bay. This guy was either the clumsiest solider in existence or had some kind of death wish.

"Okay, clearly you aren't new to this." I set the data pad down. "Let's get right to it, shall we?"

"No, I really want to keep the crystal embedded in my arm. I think it's pretty," the Skotan, Sakev, snapped again.

I stepped away from the bedside, trying to hide my annoyance.

The medical supplies were organized by species. I quickly located an unused syringe and a vial of fast-acting painkiller. I filled the syringe with the largest dosage I could give.

With any luck, it would put him to sleep as well as

numb the pain. This was the most exciting case I'd gotten since I'd come aboard.

I wanted to get it done in peace.

"This is more for me than it is for you." I quickly jabbed him with the needle.

"What was that?" He looked between me and the needle sticking out of his good arm.

"Just a little something for your pain and my peace of mind," I said with a sweet smile.

His eyelids began to flutter closed. I watched his vitals as the painkiller carried him into a state of unconscious bliss.

"That's why you shouldn't be an asshole to your doctor," I huffed as he drifted away.

SAKEV

Oh, what a wonderful feeling, I'm happy to say.

Wow. What had that woman given me?

That human song kept playing in my head over and over again. I couldn't stop it. At least my arm didn't hurt anymore, or my leg, or my back, or my head.

Do they make that stuff in canisters?

I shook my head and tried to clear my thoughts. Whatever she had shot me up with messed with my head. I didn't like it.

I noticed that she had taken the shard from my arm and placed it on a tray near me. Wasn't it blue before?

It was…I remembered.

When we fought the hybrids, the crystals on their bodies were blue, like the Xathi soldiers, but this crystal taken out of my arm was almost clear now. There was hardly any blue left to it. Weird.

She smiled down at me.

I drooled. These meds were *great!*

Then I felt a new sensation, like something biting me. I looked down to see her sticking my arm with a needle, pulling thread through the new hole she'd just put in me.

"Oh, I was hoping you'd leave that hole there. Gives me a new pocket to hide things."

The look on her face was priceless. I chuckled.

She pulled harder on the thread. It hurt.

"Okay. If you do have to stitch me up, can you at least make sure the scar looks good? Some sort of design maybe?"

"Sure. How about a pretty flower?" Her face was serious, but her tone was light.

I liked her.

She had an ethereal beauty to her.

And she was humorous.

"So the 'asshole' gets a flower?"

Vrehx's voice came from my right. "If it stops him from talking, give him a bouquet of flower-scars."

He wasn't happy with me.

I couldn't really blame him. I had acted rashly and irresponsibly. I hadn't taken the hybrids seriously enough, and it has cost all of us.

But that didn't stop me from being what the humans called snarky. "Yeah, can you stitch it like a whole, whatever he said, of flowers?"

I made my eyes wide, trying to look innocent as I asked. It sort of worked on her, because she laughed a bit as she pulled the thread a little harder, again.

"Skrell! That hurt."

It actually did. It wasn't bad pain, it was just...irritating.

Her voice came across very condescendingly as she responded to me. "Oh, I'm sorry. Did the big, bad soldier have an owie? Should I get you another shot of medicine?"

I guess I deserved that.

I shook my head, regretting it a bit as it started to hurt a little more. "No. I shall survive."

"Good. Now shut up and stop moving, or I'm going to make a mess of the stitching."

It was one of the few times that I did as I was told. I stopped moving and just watched her. I wasn't exactly the most...how would Tu'ver put it?

Subservient?

No, that wasn't the right word. I struggled to think of it, but I was never really the type to be patient and well-behaved, not unless it was absolutely necessary. But there was something about this female human that made me just sit and watch.

Her long auburn hair was pulled back into what the other females called a "pony-tail." Not sure what a pony was, but it looked good on this one. It helped to get the hair away from her eyes...those blue eyes that looked nearly black, that's how dark they were.

And the tiny little freckles on her nose were just a bit smaller than the ones on her cheekbones. They were adorable, especially on her.

She was short, too. Lying on this bed, I was still almost face-to-face with her, which meant that if I was standing, I'd tower over her like a giant.

"And...done!" She announced as she tied off my stitches and cut away the remaining thread. "Do me a favor, okay, crystal-boy? Don't screw up my stitching. I'll be back to check on your leg and back in a few when the meds have kicked in a little more."

She moved over to Vrehx and began examining his head and shoulder.

"Take care of him for me, Madam Doctor. I don't want his woman angry at me if he's scarred," I said as she began cleaning the gash on his head.

It wasn't as bad as it had originally looked, but it was still nasty to see.

"Shut up, Sakev." Vrehx was still angry at me.

"Hey, you weren't supposed to follow me. I could have handled it, if I had a few clones of myself to send in first."

He shot me a look, the one he usually gave when I needed to stop talking.

I didn't obey.

"What's your name?" I asked the comely doctor. "I'm Sakev. I'm known as the fun one in here."

"Yeah, I can tell."

Skrell. Her coldness struck home. I tried harder.

"Come on, tell me your name. Don't make me invent one for you. If I did, you probably wouldn't like it," I teased her.

Vrehx shook his head.

I could hear Tu'ver let out a grumpy sigh. Even Axtin shook his head at me.

But still I pressed on. "What? I just want to know what her name is, so I can give her a properly addressed thank-you note."

She glanced back at me, her face serious. "You really need to just rest. You're annoying the other patients."

The thing is, though, I saw her start to smile as she turned her attention back to Vrehx and his head.

"Very well. I'll rest."

A not-so-silent *about time* came from Daxion at the far side of the room. He wasn't badly hurt, just a few small scrapes. He was helping to patch up Tu'ver, whose arm still looked terribly bent the wrong way.

I watched as she finished up with Vrehx, giving him some pain medication to take and ordering him to come back and see her that evening to check the stitching. He agreed as he went to a nearby basin, washed up, and went to help Dax with Tu'ver.

There was a sickening crack as they snapped his wrist back into place. He barely grunted, but I could see the supreme effort he put into not making a sound.

She went over to check on him, running her scanner over the wrist and arm, and ordered him into a brace, so his ligaments could rest and heal. He thanked her, and she smiled at him.

It was a good smile. Not as pretty as other smiles that I had seen, but I could see that it was genuine and held a real level of care and concern in it. As she started to look at Axtin, I decided that I had rested enough.

"Come on, give me a name. Don't make me call you something unusual like...Dot, or Flower, or Stitches." I made sure to keep my tone light-hearted. I wanted her to know that I was harmless...or as harmless as a military killing machine could be.

I got nothing from her.

"Very well. I'll have to go with Stitches then. That'll fit the stitches you put in my arm, and the stitches I'll have you in when I make you laugh."

Her reply was something from my own heart. "Let me know when you say something funny, and I'll try my best to laugh."

Everyone inside the med bay laughed. I made

several different facial expressions as I nodded in defeat.

It was a good retort from her.

"That was very well done." I grinned. "I concede. I suppose I'm not as funny as I thought I was. Or maybe I haven't gotten started. But that should convince you to give me a name. Don't make me get serious about my humor."

"Oh? You weren't serious before? Okay. Give me your best shot at what you think is humor," she challenged me.

I broke out with some of my best, bringing most of team two to tears of laughter and even getting a smile out of Tu'ver.

It felt good to see him smile, but it felt so much better when I made her laugh. She visibly fought it, but she laughed several times, and that made me feel better than the pain meds did. Even General Rouhr, who was standing in a corner and monitoring things, smiled a bit.

When Stitches was done patching everyone up, Rouhr called her over.

I didn't hear everything, but I heard some of their conversation.

"He needs to stay in the med bay overnight. I'm worried about the cut to his back."

"When will he be available?"

"If things go well, he'll be back on his feet tomorrow. It's mostly a precautionary measure."

I decided to cut in. "I'm well. My back only itches a little bit." It hurt. "I'm fine."

She sucked her lips in, trying to hold back a smile.

Rouhr wasn't so nice. "Be quiet. You're lucky she's holding you in here overnight, or you'd be working in the recycling center, cleaning it up. Alone."

I stopped smiling. That was not something I wanted to do.

I *really* didn't want to be down in the recycling center. That's where everyone's…I gagged a bit.

Rouhr took advantage of my silence. "You're lucky no one was killed, and that your injuries were the only ones that were serious. If I could, I'd kick you off the team and off the ship. As of right now, you're off patrols until further notice. Let's see how *bored* you get then."

She must have seen the look on my face because she had a very sympathetic look on hers.

Later that night, as everyone else finally left, she came to check on me again. I stayed silent, letting her do her work. I rolled over, so she could check my back, which she said was good.

As she checked my arm, she smiled at me. "My name's Evangeline, but everyone calls me Evie."

She left, leaving instructions with one of the

workers playing nurse to keep an eye on my arm and to get her if anything changed. She flashed me a smile as she went to check on the others.

I laid back, smiled, and closed my eyes. It had been a long day.

Madam Doctor had somehow made this war much less boring.

EVIE

The last few hours had given me whiplash. Sakev going from rude patient to attempted charmer was hard enough to wrap my head around.

"Who knew humans were so good at pulling things out of arms?" Sakev marveled at his new line of stitches.

He was clearly still under the influence of the painkillers. I almost regretted giving him so much.

Almost, but not quite.

"Your general did." I picked up a water pouch and brought it to him. "Drink this."

"Is it poison?" he asked, wide-eyed.

"Nope." I shook my head with a chuckle. "Just water."

"A lot of people would like to poison me. I can never

be too careful." Sakev looked suspiciously around the empty room.

"I'm not one of them," I assured him.

He looked at me, eyes narrowed.

"That's what they all say. I'll drink your water. But if you poisoned it, I'm going to know. It wouldn't be the first time."

He took a slow drink.

"Really?" I asked. "You've been poisoned before?"

"Three times," he said with pride. "Though one of them was from a bad slab of roasted meat, but I'm counting it."

"Who would want to poison you?"

"Who *wouldn't* want to poison me? Even you poisoned me."

"I gave you painkillers! There's a big difference!" I exclaimed.

"If you really gave me painkillers, why does my body feel like a tree fell on me?" He polished off the water.

"Because painkillers don't last forever. You're going to be sore."

"Couldn't the pretty doctor lady give me more painkillers?" Sakev asked, and I chuckled.

"Flattery will get you far with me, but not with expensive and potentially addictive medications," I said with a mocking pout.

"Worth a shot." He shrugged, and then immediately winced.

"Try not to rip your stitches open. I worked *so* hard to make them pretty for you," I

warned. "Plus, if you do, you're going to be in a lot more pain."

"Does this stuff wear off gradually?"

"I'm not sure. In humans, we metabolize medicines gradually. But with Skotans, I don't know."

"Oh," he said through a wince. "Well, I think I just metabolized it. Skrell, that hurts."

He did seem more lucid now. I wasn't sure if that was a good thing or not. It was sort of fun sitting with a doped-up alien.

"I think full amputation would have been less cruel."

"Don't be a baby," I tutted. "You'd hate me if I took your arm. You'd hate General Rouhr, too."

"Yeah, you're right. Though I hate you both a little bit right now, anyway."

"I'm not the one who told you to charge solo into a pack of hybrids."

"Ah, you heard all of that?" Sakev asked. To his credit, he looked a little embarrassed.

"It was hard not to. Why *did* you charge in like that? You had to have known something like this could happen."

"It seemed like a good idea at the time," Sakev said defensively.

"Why do I get the feeling you say that a lot?"

I perched on the stool beside his bed and glanced at the empty med bay. Sakev was the only one who'd been ordered to stay overnight. Only the fluorescent light above his bed was still turned on.

"What are you?" Sakev narrowed his eyes. "A psychic as well as a doctor?"

"All human doctors have psychic abilities," I said smoothly.

Sakev gave me a long stare that was a mix of awe and worry.

"I'm just screwing with you." I laughed.

"You had me again. I'm impressed."

"You still have to answer the question, though." I knew he was trying to dodge the subject.

"Fine," he surrendered. "Tu'ver, the one with the busted arm, spotted four hybrids. The team couldn't decide what to do about it. They were taking too long to talk it out. People were in danger. I decided I would handle it right then and there. Four hybrids weren't a big deal. But I was ambushed. I walked right into the trap they set. The whole team paid the price."

"We know so little about the hybrids," I said. "I doubt anyone could have predicted they're sophisticated enough to plan an ambush."

"Vrehx could've. If I'd given him enough time to work it out." Sakev lowered his head. He looked defeated.

Just by looking at him, I could tell he hated being confined to the med bay. He was the sort who needed to be constantly moving. That was something we had in common.

"How's your pain?" I asked.

"My pain is a pain." A small smile appeared on his lips. "Think I could flatter you into giving me some more painkillers?"

"Not a chance," I smirked. "But I have an idea. Sit tight."

Before Sakev could ask me anything, I strode out of the med bay. As soon as I passed through the doors, my confidence faltered. I had no idea where I was.

I hadn't thought to pay attention to where I was going when I was escorted out of the refugee bay. I was in shock that had General Rouhr asked for me.

Now he was in for a surprise of his own. If I ever found his office, that is.

After several failed attempts at retracing my steps, I ended up in some sort of lounge for off-duty crew members. At least two dozen K'ver, Valorni, and Skotans stopped what they were doing to stare at me when I wandered into the room.

"This seemed like a good idea at the time," I muttered to no one in particular.

"What?" A nearby Valorni asked.

"I'm looking for General Rouhr," I spoke clearly. The crew exchanged looks as if I'd just told a joke.

"Koso. You're not going to find him in here," A Skotan snorted. A handful of others laughed before resuming their activities.

"I could use some directions." I forced a smile onto my face.

"His office is two decks up, near the bridge," a K'ver answered.

"Thanks." My smile was genuine this time.

I hurried out of the lounge to the nearest elevator. There was a map of the *Vengeance* etched into the metal, but General Rouhr's office wasn't marked. As the lift rose, I did my best to memorize as much of the ship's layout as possible.

I gasped when I stepped onto the correct deck. The bridge of the *Vengeance* looked nothing like I expected it would. Everything was sleek, streamlined, and beautiful.

The center platform's standing console projected a huge, though incomplete, map of the planet, marked with cities, known Xathi locations, and refugee camps. Data was pouring in from the ship's external scanners.

A third of the screen was dedicated to measuring

and calculating something unfamiliar to me. I could only assume the *Vengeance* was closely monitoring the rift above us.

With everything going on with the Xathi and the refugees, it was easy to forget that the rift was still open. Anything could come through.

Another, different ship had already fallen through the rift after the Xathi ship and the *Vengeance* fell through.

I didn't know much about it. Vidia told me the ship was unlike anything anyone had ever seen before. Even stranger was that it was totally abandoned.

I forced myself to focus. As much as I loved a good mystery, I'd come up here for a reason.

Now that I was on the proper deck, General Rouhr's office was easy to locate. I expected a stately room decorated with plaques and medals. While I was right about the medals and plaques, it was a cupboard of a room with just enough space for a desk and chair.

A holographic false window took up the entirety of the far wall, projecting a landscape I didn't recognize. The Skotan home world if I had to guess, but I wasn't going to ask.

"I hope I'm not disturbing you, sir," I said quietly.

General Rouhr looked up from a datapad. His brows shot up in surprised.

"Disturbed? No. But this is rather unexpected. What brings you to my office, Dr. Parr?"

He set the datapad on the desk. He seemed grateful to put it down. I doubted it contained any good news.

"I wanted to talk to you about Sakev." I was surely overstepping my bounds.

"And the surprises continue. His condition hasn't worsened, has it?"

"No." I shook my head. "In fact, he's bouncing back quicker than I anticipated. He'll be fit for duty soon."

"Shame he's on probation." General Rouhr clicked his tongue.

"That's what I wanted to talk to you about," I said quickly, before I lost my nerve. "He told me what happened. You must see that his intentions were nothing but selfless. I think his punishment might be too severe."

"I ask you for assistance once and you're already telling me how to run things on my ship?" General Rouhr's glare was withering.

"I mean no disrespect," I added hastily. "But a patient's mental state has an effect on their recovery. Keeping him off duty might have adverse effects in the future."

"On any other day I would have you escorted from my office immediately," General Rouhr warned. "But it just so happens that I have a favor I'd like to ask you. If you accept, I can make an exception for Sakev."

"A favor?" I couldn't believe it.

"I've been receiving reports from the town of Einhiv about increased hybrid activity. Paired with the reports from today's incident, it paints a concerning picture. I want you to travel to Einhiv and investigate the physical aspects of hybrids and also the potential for curing the condition. If you agree, Sakev may be your guardian."

"I accept!" If I could find a way to reverse the hybridism, it could save so many people. Even if I couldn't, I'd be out, working in my profession with people who needed me.

"You'll leave at dawn tomorrow," General Rouhr said by way of dismissal.

I practically ran back to the med bay.

Sakev sat up a little straighter when I entered.

"Go to sleep," I said excitedly. "We're going on an adventure tomorrow!"

SAKEV

I woke up in a sour mood. Rouhr had assigned me to "escort and protect" the doctor on her mission to Einhiv. Really?

I knew that I had screwed up a bit with the hybrid issue, but taking me off patrol and sticking me on bodyguard duty?

That was cruel.

With a sigh that came from my toes, I got out of bed, relieved myself, and put on my gear. I figured that I might as well take my holo belt.

The people of Einhiv might not be very hospitable to non-humans, especially after what Tu'ver told us. Better to be safe and disguised as one of them than risk emerging as an alien.

After getting dressed, making sure that my holo-disguise worked, and completing my morning meditation, I headed off for the armory. Inside, I made sure to pack a few blasters—might as well teach the doctor how to use one, just in case—and several clips for each.

I also packed three boxes of ammunition. Axtin would never let me live it down if I ran out of ammunition on a bodyguard mission.

I strapped a blaster to my hip, another to my right thigh, and hooked six clips to my belt. I placed the other blaster and three clips in a small pouch for Madam Doctor.

I then grabbed two knives. I strapped one to my left thigh and placed the other in the pouch. I finished off our weapons cache with a small selection of neuro-grenades and my two swords.

While the swords weren't the most useful against the Xathi, they worked fantastically well against the local plant life and hybrids. Even if I didn't need them, I'd carry them around. I'd rather carry them around for nothing than need them and not have them.

I checked the time and realized that I had enough of it to get myself some food. On the way down to the galley, I called down to the hangar and arranged for a hover carrier to transport the doctor and myself.

Why spend forever walking, when we can get there quickly? The added bonus was that the hover team would be able to conduct a patrol while flying us to Einhiv and back. At least the trip out there wouldn't be a complete waste of time.

I made it to the galley and fixed myself some breakfast. I also packed some rations for our trip, as well. It wouldn't do to go hungry.

I ate a fantastic dish that the human ladies had introduced us to. They called them pancakes. Along with some scrambled eggs and a nice thick slab of meat, this was a fantastic way to start an otherwise dreary morning.

I was halfway through my meal when the doctor came in.

"Morning!"

She seemed to be a bit too cheery this morning, but after finding out that she hadn't left the ship since we rescued her several months ago, I could understand the enthusiasm.

With a mouth full of food, I nodded to her.

"Morning to you as well, doctor," I finally said after swallowing my bite of pancake. With—what was it called?—strawberry jelly on the pancakes, it was like getting a small bite of paradise between every bite of perfection with my meat and eggs.

"I see you're eating healthy this morning, steak and eggs with some pancakes. You really like those pancakes, don't you?" She grabbed her own pancakes, some eggs of her own, and something she called yogurt.

I couldn't stand the yogurt stuff personally. It smelled like rotten fruit to me, and I was sure it tasted similar.

"What can I say? You humans are pretty good at creating foods. The pure unhealthiness of these things makes them perfect." I smiled at her as she sat down. "Are you ready to go?"

She took some pepper from the center of the table, sprinkled it on her eggs, and returned it. "As soon as we're done eating. I heard you arranged transport for us?"

"How did you hear that?"

She smiled as she bit into her eggs. "I was already in the hangar when you called it in. I was double checking Tu'ver's injuries."

She looked around as if she was missing something, then with a nod of comprehension, she got up and headed over to the replicator. She got herself something to drink. She looked back at me with a questioning gaze and, at my nod, got me a glass of her juice as well.

"Thank you," I mumbled with a full mouth.

She shook her head as she sat back down. "Pig."

"What?" I had no idea what a "pig" was, so I wasn't sure if I had just been insulted or not.

"Nothing. Let's eat. We need to get there soon."

"Whatever you say, Madam Doctor," I said with a smirk.

She looked at me, maybe slightly hurt, maybe not. I couldn't tell. "You don't have to call me 'Madam Doctor,' you know. I'm okay with Evie. It is my name, after all."

I dipped my head a bit in apology. "I was just trying to be polite. Didn't want to mess up that fantastic connection we established yesterday when you stabbed me."

She choked on her pancakes. It was worth it. After clearing her throat, she looked at me in mock shock.

"'Stabbed you?' I gave you some pain meds so I could fix you up. Besides, that was a tiny little needle."

"Tiny? It was massive!"

We spent the rest of breakfast disagreeing about the size of the weapon she used and even talked about it on the way to the hangar bay.

We boarded the hover carrier and sat down, then she noticed the pouch I was carrying and asked about it.

I handed it to her. "It's yours."

"Mine?" She raised her eyebrows.

"In case something happens...a blaster, some ammunition, and a knife."

She backed away from me, declining the pouch with a vehement shake of her head. "No. No, I don't want those things."

"You might need them. If something happens where I can't protect you, it'll be good to be armed," I argued as I held the pouch out to her. "I'll show you how to load the blaster and use it. Hopefully, you won't have to, but it's always better to be prepared."

She looked at me for a moment before reluctantly agreeing.

I walked her through how to power-up the blaster, how to fire it, and how to change the clips on it as we were flown to Einhiv. It wasn't a long trip, since we were located only a few dozen miles away.

Einhiv would have been a beautiful city if it wasn't so heavily guarded. With many of the buildings built in concert with the surrounding forest, Einhiv looked to almost be part of the nature surrounding it.

That is, until you looked at the outskirts of the town. They had erected some crudely-built but reasonably thick walls and had placed as many weapons around the walls as they could. Men and women patrolled the walls with rifles, as well as some of the outer streets.

The town's air command signaled us on our commlink, demanding to know our intentions.

We received clearance to fly past the walls but were not permitted to land.

"We need to land to be able to do anything," Evie said to herself in disgust before turning to the pilot. "Patch me through."

A second later, the commlink was activated.

"My name is Evangeline Parr. I'm a doctor, here to help with the reported hybrid activity in the area." She made a passionate plea, but I wasn't sure it would matter.

The voice on the other end of the comms came back after a few seconds of hesitation. "We apologize Dr. Parr, but we have no knowledge of who you are, therefore we cannot verify your intentions. To be honest, you're lucky we let your craft inside the city walls. Now, if you don't mind, please vacate the area and return to wherever you came from."

She looked at the pilot of our hover carrier, then at me. "I can't believe they're turning me down."

She got back on the comm and tried again. "I'm one of the few survivors from Fraga, and I want to help deal with the hybrid Xathi issue that I've been hearing about. I swear, I'm only here to help."

"Miss, I'm sorry, I really am. I had family in Fraga.

But, and I only say this out of necessity, we cannot allow your craft to land. Now, as a final act of politeness before we order our gunners to shoot you down, please vacate the area and leave us be." The comms turned off.

Evie looked at me. I could see the loss in her face, and that made me angry. When she said that we should go ahead and leave, I had had enough.

"Sorn," I said to the pilot, "take us slowly over the roof of that building to your left. When we're out, get back to the *Vengeance* quickly. Got it?"

He nodded and turned the carrier around slowly.

"What are you doing?" Evie asked.

"Getting us into the city, what else? You ready?" I shouldered my pack.

"What the hell do you mean?"

"We're jumping down onto the roof. They might not want our help right now, but they need it. So...let's help."

Her eyes went wide. "Jumping?!"

"Well," I said as I took a step towards her, "to be more precise, I'm jumping. You're just going along for the ride."

As she opened her mouth to say something, I smacked the button to open the bay doors, activated my holo-disguise, scooped her up, and jumped out of the carrier.

Sorn had gotten us within only a few feet of the

roof, so it wasn't a far distance. I barely had to bend my knees as we landed.

I ducked us down as the carrier took off, the bay doors closing as it flew away.

I smiled down at Evie, not exactly sure why she was scowling at me.

EVIE

"What the hell is wrong with you?" I screamed, wiggling out of Sakev's grip.

"I think you mean, 'Thank you, Sakev! You've allowed the mission to continue!'" He flashed a grin. My distress amused him.

"Seriously, don't you think *anything* through?" I threw my hands in the air.

"You wanted to get into the city. We're in the city. What's the problem?"

Sakev surveyed the roof. There was no obvious doorway down to lower levels. I assumed he was looking for a hatch or something.

While he was looking around, I walked to the edge of the building and peered over. Residents of Einhiv were rushing towards the building, visibly armed and pissed off.

"The problem is you've ticked off the locals." I backed away from the edge. I could hear the shouts of the crowd forming below us.

"I agree, that's a problem." Sakev rubbed the back of his neck. "But it's not our biggest problem."

"What?" I clenched my jaw. "What's our biggest problem?"

"Looks like the only way down is to scale down the side of the building." Sakev knelt down and retrieved a length of rope and a harness from his backpack.

"You're oddly prepared for this," I snarked.

"Scaling down tall buildings is fun." Sakev clipped himself into the harness. "Come here, I'll clip you in."

"You're out of your mind."

I backed away. I'd almost reached the edge of the roof once more. A shot rang out from below, ricocheting off the side of the building and sending me scurrying away from the ledge.

This was not what I had in mind when I agreed to help Rouhr.

What kind of lunatics refuse professional medical help in the middle of a war?

"If you have a better idea, I'm all ears," Sakev shot back as he secured the rope.

My mind raced. There had to be something better than this.

"Damn it! Fine. But be careful with your holo-disguise. They'll shoot you for sure if they see you aren't human."

"But my scales are so lovely in the sunlight," Sakev jested.

"I'm tempted to let them shoot you."

"You're a hostile little thing, you know that?"

"I'm sorry I'm not more personable after being thrown onto a roof and surrounded by people with weapons who don't want us here," I snapped.

"What's your excuse for every other time?"

I glared at him.

"Next time you're on a medical bed—"

"So, a few hours from now?" Sakev cut me off.

I laughed, despite myself. He was funny, no denying that.

"Exactly. I'm not giving you painkillers," I finished.

"I can take it." He smirked.

With a flick of the wrist, he activated his disguise. His skin shimmered, and in the blink of an eye, he transformed. His eyes were still honey-colored, and his hair was still brown, but his skin turned deep gold, like he worked under the sun for a living.

An odd feeling ran through me. It was a hell of a sight…but it wasn't him.

"Do you approve, Madam Doctor?" He winked.

I scowled.

"The technology is impressive. Humans are years from creating a holograph that sits on the skin like that." I looked at anything but Sakev.

"Don't be embarrassed, Madam Doctor. I think you're cute, too."

I rolled my eyes.

"Ready to do this?" He swung the rope that was meant to hold both of our weights.

"Now's as good a time as ever." I shuddered.

"Climb on my back, then." Sakev crouched down, allowing me to scramble onto his back.

I clung to his broad shoulders and locked my legs around his waist. He clipped the rope to one of my beltloops, then stood up.

"Look at that." He twisted his head to look at me sideways. "You're the perfect size to shield against blasters and bullets."

"Oh, hell no." I wiggled against the rope but I was tightly secured on Sakev's back.

"Relax." Sakev laughed. "I'm only kidding. I'm really good at dodging blaster shots."

"Was that supposed to make me feel better?"

"Did it not?" Sakev checked the knot attached to the pipe sticking out of the roof one more time before stepping up to the ledge.

"Nothing about this situation is making me feel good."

I cast a wary eye to the ground below. It would be a fatal fall.

I found myself subconsciously clinging tighter to Sakev. The people below us lifted their weapons. I heard the hum of several blasters powering up.

Sakev swung us over the edge before I could react. The people below us started firing.

"Well, clearly they aren't military," Sakev mused. "They can't aim for skrell."

"Please, don't shoot!" I begged. "We're human! I'm a doctor! We came to offer aid!"

"Hold your fire," a distant voice came from below. Relief flooded me as the blasters went silent.

"Very good," Sakev grunted as he pushed off the side of the building with his legs. I kept my eyes skyward, refusing to look down. "You're really digging in those nails of yours."

"Oh, I'm sorry," I hissed. "I'm just a little nervous."

"Last night you were so excited to go on an adventure. What changed?"

"I prefer the sort of adventures where I'm not immediately faced with my own mortality."

"You're joking! Those are the best kind of adventures," Sakev argued.

"When we get on the ground, we need to have a serious talk about your priorities."

More than anything, I wanted to look down just to see how much longer I'd be strapped to the back of a moron with no sense of self-preservation.

"Don't do it." Sakev startled me. My head snapped back to a forward position. "If you look down, you're only going to disorient yourself."

"How did you know—"

"I can feel every little move you make. Did you forget you're strapped to my back?"

Sakev pushed off the wall again, lowering us down another few feet, but when his boots came into contact with the wall, it gave way. His grip loosened for less than a second, but it was long enough for us to slip and for me to be thrown dangerously off balance.

I tightened my grip around his neck, hiding my face. If we hurtled toward the ground, I didn't want to see it.

"I'm sure you know this, but most lifeforms need to breathe to function," he rasped, and I loosened my grip.

"How long does it take you to scale down a damn building?" My voice was tight.

Tears welled in my eyes but I willed them away. I forced myself to take steady breaths. Sakev did this sort of reckless stuff all the time, and, surprisingly, he'd managed to live this long.

"Not as long as it would take you, I bet," Sakev shot back.

"Please, just get us on the ground as quick as you can."

"Understood."

Sakev shoved off the wall again. We dropped ten feet with each push. I tried to ignore the feeling of my stomach flipping around.

Once on the ground, we were instantly surrounded by men in official uniforms of Einhiv. Thankfully, they'd stowed their weapons.

"Identify yourselves immediately," an official with a bushy moustache demanded.

"I'm Dr. Evangeline Parr. This is my associate Sakev...Smith," I said quickly.

I'd get an earful from Sakev later. "We were working in Kaster. We heard talk that this city was struggling. We're here to help."

"Who told you we were struggling?" I didn't miss the suspicion on the official's face.

"It's common knowledge that every city is struggling right now." I mustered a confused laugh.

"Sir." Another official came forward with a datapad. "Dr. Evangeline Parr checks out. She's legitimate. We couldn't find any record of a Sakev Smith."

"And why might that be?" the moustache official asked me.

"Is it against a law for a man to remake himself for a better life?" Sakev piped up.

I tried not to let my shock register on my face. Where had that come from?

"Mr. Smith has been my personal bodyguard for years," I supplied quickly. "He's been thoroughly vetted. I trust him with my life."

"The feeling is mutual, Madam Doctor," Sakev preened.

I gave him a warning look concealed under a smile.

"That still doesn't explain why you're here," the official said.

"You heard her. She wants to help and the good doctor enlisted me to protect her. There is a war going on, you know?" Sakev said.

I wanted to elbow him, but I couldn't think of a way to do it subtly.

"Yes," the official said gruffly. "We're aware. That's why we've placed extra security measures. Security measures you made a point of ignoring."

"Our shuttle driver went a bit rogue on us." Sakev shrugged. "He wasn't going to take us all the way back to Kaster. We didn't have much of a choice."

"What kind of shuttle was that, exactly? I've never seen anything like it before."

"How should I know?" Sakev replied. "It was his personal vehicle. He probably built it himself."

"Why—"

"Look, if you don't want us here, we'll respect that. Organize a shuttle to take us back to Kaster, and we'll leave you in peace. Hopefully, the residents won't be too upset that city officials turned down one of the best doctors on the planet."

Sakev spoke loudly and clearly. The nearby locals certainly heard him. They all looked at me with interest and even a glimmer of hope.

"Excuse me. I have to confer with my superiors." The official strode away, speaking rapidly into his commlink.

"My plan worked perfectly," Sakev said with a mocking bow.

"To call their bluff?" I guessed.

Sakev shook his head, looking entirely too pleased with himself.

"That wasn't planned, but it was a spectacular performance on my part."

"What plan?" My eyes narrowed in suspicion.

"To keep you angry and annoyed with me, so you wouldn't get scared," he grinned at me.

I didn't know what to say. I didn't expect a gesture like that from him.

It was…sweet.

"Dr. Parr." The official returned. "You will be escorted to the city clinic. Mr. Smith, since we cannot verify your identity, we will have to take you to a holding cell for safety evaluation."

Sakev was silent as they led us away, but I could see his lips move.

I heard one word, and I smiled.

"Skrell."

SAKEV

Perhaps saying things went in an unfortunate direction was an understatement.

I sat captive as a prisoner in a holding cell because the humans in this small agricultural town didn't trust me.

It was insulting.

My holo-disguise covered up my real skin, making me look like a massive human instead. Also, I did jump out of the carrier after they told us to leave, but still... how could they not trust *me*?

Of course, Evie loved the whole thing. She teased me about it incessantly.

"I told you. Didn't I tell you not to be an asshole?"

I looked at her through the bars of my cell.

"When did you tell me that?"

"When I *stabbed* you back in the med bay. I warned you not to be an asshole, but you just had to say something, didn't you?"

She was sitting in a chair, arms crossed, a smile plastered on her freckled face, as my *guards* were dealing with the paperwork and waiting for word on what they should do with me.

"I'm sorry. I didn't realize that talking was a terrible thing. Why don't you do some *talking* and get me out of here?"

She laughed. "I don't know. You behind bars, almost look like you belong there or something."

If only she knew.

She turned her attention to the guards, talking over her shoulder. "Any idea how long he'll be in there?"

The smaller of the two guards, a man that looked to be somewhere in his forties, was the one to answer.

"Not entirely sure, ma'am. The two of you *were* ordered to leave, yet here you are. To be honest," he said as he looked up, "both of you should be in there. But the people, and our bosses, seem to trust you." He pointed at her as he finished the sentence.

Then he shifted his finger towards me, "You? Not so much."

"Why not?" I asked.

"Your friend here is right. If you hadn't opened your mouth, it might not have been an issue."

Evie snorted. "Told you so."

I shook my head and sat down on the bunk, completely dejected. I hated being locked up.

I needed to move. I needed to do things. I needed to be out of this cell. I looked up, to see Evie looking at me.

I turned away from her, hating the look on her face.

"Hey."

I looked up.

Evie stood at the door to my cell, her hands on the bars. "I'll get you out of here."

With a sneer in my voice, I asked. "Yeah? How?"

"Let me go make nice with some of the officials. Maybe I can convince them that you're my bodyguard *and* my assistant. I'll be back soon, okay?"

"Praise Skotan," I said sarcastically.

I was angry—at her, at the situation, at the fools that had locked me up, at Rouhr for making me her sitter.

Evie walked away, leaving me to sit in this ridiculously tiny cell with those two idiots out there to *guard* me.

The cell really was small. It was barely bigger than I was each way.

The bed, to be honest, was too small for me. I tried to lie down, but my legs dangled off the end of the bunk right about where my knees began. That made my calves very uncomfortable.

I leaned back against the wall, using my arm as a pillow, and thought about what had happened since we came through the rift.

I must have dozed off. My two guards were... arguing? About me, from the sounds of it.

"I'm telling you, he's one of those aliens we've heard about!"

The voice wasn't familiar, so it must have been the younger one. I racked my brain to remember what he looked like—a few inches shorter than me, skinny, pimple-faced...either very young or hadn't seen a shower in months if his face was covered in pimples. I had hated those when I was a child, embarrassing to have.

"How do you know he's one of them aliens?" That was the older guard, the one that had answered Evie's question earlier.

"I saw them when they jumped. His skin was red, like bright red."

Skrell.

"Really? Doesn't look red to me. Couldn't you have just imagined the red skin?"

"No! He was red, I swear he was. We need to get rid of him." I didn't particularly like the sound of that. If it meant what I thought it meant, he wanted me dead. I rather liked being not dead.

The older one responded. "Whoa, hold on there, kid. We can't just kill him. What if he's human, like we are?"

"What if he's not?" the young one countered.

The older one grunted in exasperation. "Look, just because he's an ass doesn't mean he's an alien. If being a total ass makes you an alien, then most of us would be in that category. Just let it be."

"Oh my god. I didn't say he was an alien because he's a jerk," the guard countered. "I said that he had red skin! No human has red skin. He's one of those damn aliens, I tell you. We need to kill the thing."

"No, Drew! What the hell are you thinking? We can't kill him."

"Why not?"

This was too much.

"Because I didn't do anything wrong!" I yelled through the bars.

The two guards came around the corner to look at me. The older one seemed to be more sympathetic towards me, while Drew glared at me.

It was Drew that spoke up. "Shut up, you alien scumbag! It's your fault things are going so badly here. Every single one of you should be killed to fix the problem."

I had had enough. If he wanted to kill me, he'd better come get in my face and do it like a real male.

"Really? You think you can kill me? Then get over

here and try it, you miserable excuse for a fool," I taunted him.

HE REACHED FOR HIS WEAPON, but the older one grabbed his arm and shook his head. Drew yanked his arm away and approached the cell.

"Not very smart of you to antagonize me. You don't have any weapons, or anywhere to hide."

I pressed my face against the bars. "I'd wager that you could put your gun right against my skull and you'd still miss."

Drew yelled at me and rushed the cell. I stepped back as he unlocked the door, pushing the older guard to the ground when he tried to stop him. He unholstered his weapon and pointed it at me, his hand shaking.

I laughed at him. "You can't do it, can you? That's why your hand is shaking so much. You've never shot anyone before, have you? You're just a coward with a badge and a gun!"

Drew's face was red. He was barely holding on. The older guard tried to tell him to calm down, but it seemed as though the older man's words only made Drew angrier.

I pushed the moment.

I stepped closer to him, letting a short snarl escape

my lips.

"Coward!" I growled. "You want to shoot me, don't you? It's not that hard. You just squeeze the trigger. But you must hold the weapon steady. Like this!"

I snapped my hand forward, ripping the gun from his hand, turning it, and pointing it in his face. The gun didn't move. It was as steady as a statue.

"See that? No movement, no shake. All I have to do is squeeze the trigger and the insides of your head decorate that wall behind you."

Drew's face had gone from a deep crimson to an amazing shade of pale. I sniffed something, then looked at him in wonder and disgust.

"I think you just excreted on yourself, don't you?" I asked with a smirk.

I shook my head. It figured. I hadn't meant to scare him that bad, just wanted to stop him from talking about killing me. I tried to diffuse the situation.

"Apologies for the heavy-handedness of what I've done. And," looking at the older guard, "I can be a bit of an asshole, as you say. It's just part of who I am. I don't mean to upset anyone or offend anyone. Can we just let this go and you let me out of here? I'm really not a fan of closed-in spaces."

I never thought Drew had it in him. He dove at me, grabbing the gun as he punched me in the face. It wasn't much of a punch, but the surprise of the blow rocked my head back.

I brought my head down and stared at him, a not-so-happy look on my face. His eyes went wide for a split second before my head snapped forward, forehead crashing into his. He hit the floor with a loud thud, unconscious.

I looked at Drew, then over at the older guard.

He was looking between me and Drew, absorbing the situation. He settled his gaze on me as he took a hesitant step forward, his hand on his weapon.

With a heavy sigh, I flipped Drew's gun around so that I held it by the barrel. I held it out to the guard.

"I just want to go to where the doctor is, that's all. I'm really not a problem, even if I talk like one." I tried to dial up a reassuring smile.

It must have worked. The guard released his own weapon, stepped forward, and slowly took Drew's weapon from my hand. "You promise to be on your best behavior?"

"Yes, sir."

"Fine. I'll take you to her. Just don't do anything stupid, okay?"

"You have my word."

EVIE

"Are there many doctors available within the city?" I asked the official escorting me to the clinic.

"Not right now," he said. "Most of our top medical professionals went to Duvest to offer their services. It seemed like the prudent course of action at the time. Then the troubles here started."

To my surprise, the clinic was set up in an actual hospital. The large lobby was divided into sections with sheets and curtains, not unlike my own office back on the *Vengeance*. But, as far as I could tell, patients were only being seen in the lobby.

"Why not utilize the entire hospital?" I asked.

"Those things beyond the wall took out our generators. We have backups, but they aren't as powerful. We shut down the hospital equipment that drains the most power. Most of the injuries we see here are work-related. Einhiv is the agricultural capital, after all."

I wanted to ask more questions about the hybrids, but I was hesitant to reveal how much I knew.

The officials and residents were already distrustful of outsiders. If they knew I was allied with the aliens, even if they were the good ones, they would evict me from the city. With no shuttle to take me back to the *Vengeance*, I'd be at the mercy of the hybrids.

And there was still the matter of Sakev. I figured the best way to earn his release was to help out as much as I could. Currying favor with the residents and the officials could only help at that point. Once Sakev was freed, he and I could set out to do what we came here for.

I took a moment to look around. I located the supply stores and got an idea of what sort of treatments I could offer. At least Einhiv was still well stocked with basic medical supplies.

Hopefully, I wouldn't run into anything more serious than a laceration or mild illness.

I decided to focus on the small cluster of children and parents first. Most of the cases were easy. Routine checkups scheduled before the hybrids came and made life more difficult.

There were a few small scrapes here and there that just needed to be cleaned and bandaged. I wished I had something to give the kids, like candy or a little trinket.

One would need more care. He'd accidently caught his arm on a piece of scrap metal and required stitches, as his mother explained to me. The only problem was, the kid wouldn't come near me.

I didn't know what to do. I'd never been very good with children.

Calixta was different. I viewed her as a niece, or the child of a dear friend.

A child I didn't know was a completely different story.

"It's so comforting to see how hard you're fighting to get me out." My spine went ramrod straight at Sakev's voice.

"Excuse me for one moment, would you?" I mustered my sweetest voice.

Confused, the parent nodded and went back to attempting to reason with her ornery child.

"How?" I demanded once I was out of earshot.

"I had a little chat with my keepers," Sakev said smugly.

"And they let you walk out?"

"I'm here, aren't I? No thanks to you," Sakev teased. I knew he was trying to rattle me for his own amusement.

"I was busy making nice with the locals that you pissed off," I reminded him. "I was going to ask them to release you once they trusted me a little more."

"Well, I beat you to it. What can I do to help?" He asked. I blinked in surprise.

"Really? You want to help?"

"Is that so hard to believe?" Sakev almost sounded hurt.

"Are you good with kids?" I asked. Sakev's eyes lit up. Without another word to me, he walked over to the child who'd been uncooperative earlier.

"You want to see something you will never forget?" Sakev asked the frightened child in a soft voice I hadn't heard him use. And I worried.

What on earth did he have in mind?

The kid didn't answer, but he didn't shy away when Sakev knelt down next to him. He rolled up his sleeve to show the kid a scar on his forearm that looked like a star burst.

My mind automatically went into overdrive. I knew the holographic disguises kept the general shape and form of the wearer. But to be so refined as to display and modify scars or birthmarks... the technology was amazing.

I blushed as I speculated upon what other scars Sakev had hidden?

"Whoa!" The kid gasped. "How'd you get that?"

"I was trying to make a micro-grenade and it backfired. Literally," Sakev explained.

"What's the point of a micro-grenade?" I laughed.

"Only someone with no imagination would ask that." Sakev made a show of looking offended.

"You're a terrible influence," I sighed.

"Did it hurt?" The kid asked Sakev.

"Not too bad. And if this didn't hurt, then what Madam Doctor needs to do is to make sure you're healthy. It's not going to be that bad, right?"

"I guess." The child shuffled his way over to me. I examined the gash on his arm.

"Once we clean this up, I'll be able to see if you need stitches or not," I explained.

"Give me a cool scar like he has!" The kid excitedly pointed to Sakev.

"Now look what you've done." I gave Sakev a playfully stern look.

He grinned in return. I didn't expect this from him.

Watching him entertain the child was…charming. He kept the other children laughing with crazy stories while I worked. He even took it upon himself to talk to the parents before sending the kids to me.

When he wasn't being a total ass, Sakev and I worked well together.

Who would've thought?

We'd finished treating the last child and were preparing to move on to other patients when we heard shouting and the sound of breaking glass from the front of the building.

"That doesn't sound good." I moved in the direction of the sound, fearing a medical emergency the clinic was unprepared for. Sakev grabbed my arm, holding me back.

"I don't think it's a new patient, Evie," Sakev said in a low voice. His serious tone threw me off, as well as calling me by my name.

Sakev knew something was wrong.

A group of men made their way through the lobby, knocking over tables of supplies and threatening patients as they moved.

"What the hell are they doing?" I tried to move forward once more, but Sakev gripped me harder.

"Let me handle this. They're armed," Sakev warned. For once, I nodded in agreement.

I moved behind him when the group approached us. The man I assumed to be their leader was only a few inches shorter than Sakev and was built like a brick wall.

"What seems to be the problem here?" Sakev asked, his voice calm and collected.

"Our buddy Drew told us a *real* interesting story

about you." The man lumbered closer, smacking the lead pipe he carried against his palm.

"You couldn't stay quiet, could you, Drew?" Sakev muttered.

"Who the hell is Drew?" I asked, more confused than ever. "How did you manage to piss off this many people in such a short time? You were locked in a *cell!*"

"What can I say? It's an art form I've mastered," Sakev replied.

"Your artistry is going to get us killed," I snapped.

"These guys broke in and started smashing up the clinic and you're blaming my sarcasm?" Sakev had the nerve to look shocked.

"No, I'm blaming your uncanny ability to make people angry, including myself!"

"You enjoy it." Sakev flashed me a grin that would have been devastatingly attractive if we weren't in immediate danger. "I'll take care of this. You worry about your patients and your equipment."

"Oddly enough, I don't find that comforting," I said to his back as he walked toward the angry group.

"All you're doing here is hurting your own people." Sakev tried to reason with the group. I watched him as I tried to reassure the nervous patients.

"We aren't too fond of outsiders around here," the leader said.

"Even doctors?" Sakev asked.

"I wasn't talking about the doctor. Though, if you ask me, she's way too pretty to be a doctor," the man sneered. His eyes roved over my body. I shuddered in disgust.

"I didn't ask. And you should refrain from speaking about her like that." Though Sakev's voice was calm, I could hear the anger behind it.

I'd never seen him in combat, but I'd heard stories.

Skotans were formidable in a fight, especially with their retractable scales. If this turned violent, would Sakev risk revealing himself by using his scales?

Would the disguise cover them, or let them show, like the scar?

"You should watch your mouth, scum. We know what you are." The man pointed his pipe at Sakev's chest.

Sakev only smirked.

"Oh, that's right. Drew convinced himself I'm an alien," he laughed. He spread his arms, putting his disguised body on display. "I guess Drew sees anyone bigger and stronger than him as an alien, huh?" He spoke loudly, drawing the attention of almost everyone in the lobby.

Everyone was looking him over and seeing that there was nothing alien about him whatsoever. I held my breath, hoping no one knew anything.

"Drew isn't a liar," the man with the pipe hissed.

"Maybe he is. Maybe he isn't. But he is a coward. If he wasn't, he'd be standing next to you instead of counting on you to take out his enemies."

Sakev folded his broad arms across his chest. His arm muscles strained the fabric of his shirt. The group looked unsure of themselves.

I released a breath.

"That's what I thought." Sakev turned his back on them and began to walk away. That was his mistake. The man with the pipe lunged the moment Sakev took his eyes off him.

"Look out!" I shouted. Sakev dodged, the pipe narrowly missing his head.

"Big mistake," he growled as the man attacked again.

He must have been military, or ex-military. He definitely knew how to fight. But so did Sakev.

It took only a few seconds for Sakev to disarm his attacker, but the rest of the group quickly closed in.

I moved quickly, ushering all the patients as far away from the fight as I could get them. When I turned my attention back to the brawl, three of the attackers were on the floor, knocked out cold.

The man that started it all drew a knife. He lunged at Sakev while Sakev was fighting off two others. I wanted to scream, but I was paralyzed with fear.

Faster than I thought possible, Sakev swung the pipe into the man's jaw.

There was a sickening crack as his neck broke.

Skrell.

SAKEV

To say my judgment was erroneous would've been charity.

Evie told me not to interfere, but I did anyway.

They were trying to destroy the clinic, what was I supposed to do? I couldn't just sit there. That wasn't part of my nature.

There was no way I would be able to just sit back and let the clinic be destroyed.

So, I got involved, tried to save the clinic, and someone ended up dead.

Dead by my hands while I hadn't meant to kill anyone, it just happened in the heat of battle. Then the guards and other town officials finally got involved and broke up the fight.

I was left to answer for it all.

I sat on the bunk in the same cell that I'd been in before. Drew had been reassigned, the older guard had been given the day off, and Evie was arguing with town officials on my behalf...again. It made me wonder if she was better off without me.

I could hear Evie's voice as she pled my case. "You do realize that if he hadn't been there, the clinic would've been destroyed and more people would've been hurt, right?"

I didn't know the voice that spoke next, but it was female, and old. "Yes, we do. However, he killed someone. Are we supposed to ignore that fact?"

No, don't ignore it, but it was in defense of the clinic and the people, I thought to myself as she said the words.

"You're right, you can't ignore it," Evie said. "But don't ignore the fact that it was in self-defense. Sakev didn't intend to kill anyone while defending the clinic and the people inside."

Well, well, well.

Evie and I just happened to think alike.

"We understand that," came the old voice. "We truly do. And please understand that while we don't condone murder or death, we also don't believe in condemning anyone for something beyond their control. However, your young man back there looks very much capable of handling himself. I assume he's had military training, which also means he should be able to restrain himself from anything that results in death."

I SENSED Evie's frustration before her voice confirmed it. "Really? He can control every single thing that happens in a fight? Have you ever been in a fight?"

"No, I'm proud to say that I haven't."

"Then how in the holy hell would you know anything about controlling what happens in a fight? You can't control what your opponent is going to do, or how they're going to react. If you could, there wouldn't be a damn fight in the first place!"

Damn, she said exactly what I was thinking.

Then the old voice spoke up again. "Dr. Parr, please calm down. You're not helping your friend back there."

"Calm down?! Really? You're trying to tell me that he had control over that idiot in the clinic, yet you've never been in a fight, so you have no idea how a fight works. I was in a few growing up. I had older brothers...you can't control your opponent. You have no control over their actions, or their reactions. The fact that Sakev killed someone is an unfortunate, terrible thing, but he didn't *mean* to kill anyone. If he hadn't stepped in to defend the clinic, that group of rabid morons would have torn the clinic apart and hurt a lot more people inside before your *crack* squad of guards arrived."

"Miss—" the old lady was cut off by a different voice. I couldn't hear what they said, but it seemed to end whatever argument she had.

"I see," she finally said. "Dr. Parr, we need to speak with your friend."

"Fine."

I heard the footsteps of at least five, maybe six, people coming down the hall towards my cell. I was right, it was an old lady that Evie was arguing with. She must have been in her seventies, her age betrayed by her silver hair and wrinkled face.

She wore the same badge as the three guards that followed, all of whom were in their standard blue uniform and stood at attention when they stopped moving. They respected her and seemed to defer to her for everything.

Evie walked next to her, not at all happy with what was going on.

The last person, number six, was ridiculously young…maybe sixteen…but was dressed like an official. The suit was tailor-made for the child, and his shoes brightly reflected the lights above. His hair was parted to the side and slicked down with some sort of chemical to hold it in place.

He carried himself with purpose, almost as if he was

someone important.

That kind of ridiculous confidence amused me.

So, of course, I decided to annoy him.

"I'd like to lodge a small complaint about my living arrangements," I began. "You see, the bunk is far too comfortable, and the lavatory is far too private, not nearly embarrassing enough for me."

Evie's face fell as I spoke. She mouthed for me to stop, but I was too far in and continued. "Also, the food here is terrible. Granted, I haven't had anything to eat yet, but I'd assume it was bad." I smiled.

So did the old lady.

The child did not. "I see you like to be funny," he said, a scowl on his face.

I shrugged and winked at him. "Eh."

He "harrumphed" at me and turned to the old lady. "Madam Raschke, I believe that it is time for this man to go. His time in Einhiv is over."

"Whoa, hold on a minute," Evie said, cutting the old lady off. "If he leaves, I leave. We're a package deal."

Awww, she cares. She likes me, she really likes me! I thought as I flashed her my most sincere smile.

I stuck my tongue out at the kid.

He glared at me.

With a grin, Madam Raschke spoke up. "No offense, Dr. Parr, why should it matter if you stay or not?"

One of the guards cleared his throat as he raised his hand a bit.

Everyone looked at him like a statue had just moved on its own. "I mean no disrespect, Madam Raschke, or to you either, Mr. Drayton, but our only remaining doctor was injured in the last attack. Dr. Parr is currently the only person with the appropriate medical experience needed to deal with our injured, at least until Doctor Larkin is back on his feet. Ma'am. Sir."

He took a deep breath after he was done. I wasn't sure if he'd never spoken before in his life and that's why he didn't know he was allowed to breathe, or if talking to these two people was that scary for him.

"You mean to tell me that there is no one else that can put on a bandage or hand out a pain med?" the child, Mr. Drayton, asked. His voice was a bit high-pitched when he spoke. He might've been a bit perturbed.

I gave him a big toothy smile and a thumbs-up when he turned to look at me. He rolled his eyes and turned away.

I shrugged at Evie. "I tried," I said quietly.

"Your volunteers are med-students," Evie answered. "They're bright and willing, but are you willing to risk having only students in charge of the hospital?"

Madam Raschke grinned at me, then looked at Mr. Drayton. "Sir, we do need her help, at least for the next day or two. And if she needs him," she said as she jerked a thumb at me, "then maybe he should stay."

"We'll assign her guards," he answered, scowling.

"Oh, hell no, you won't!" Evie yelled.

She was glorious when angry.

"I don't feel safe here without him. Your guards, no offense towards you three," she said with a quick nod at the guards, "have shown that they can't handle this anti-alien group that's running around. I'm sorry, but I don't have any faith in your guards to protect me and keep me safe. If Sakev is not allowed to stay, then I'm leaving with him."

There was silence. "Let's see you," she emphasized that last word as she stuck her finger in Drayton's face, "try to take care of the sick and hurt people here. Let's see you get a little dirty."

He smacked her finger away from his face, which drew a small growl from me. He looked at me, a fancy little smirk that I wanted so desperately to wipe off his face with my boot.

"If he does anything, and I do mean anything, that upsets a single person in this town, I will have the two of you thrown out of Einhiv. Is that clear?" He walked away before anyone was able to answer.

Madam Raschke watched him leave, then turned back to us. "I guess that means you're allowed to stay." She turned to me, "Will you behave?"

I put on a look of mock shock as I answered. "Have I not so far?"

Evie's head dropped. I might've taken the humor a bit too far.

"Uh, huh." Madam Raschke turned to Evie. "Is he good at anything besides bodyguard duty? Do you really need him?"

Before Evie could answer, I spoke up. I used my serious voice this time. "I'm actually pretty good with weapons. I've even successfully field tested some tech that works well against the Xathi. I might be persuaded to share the tech." Evie looked at me in total shock. I knew I had forgotten to mention something to her.

Madam Raschke turned towards me, one hand on her hip. She had definitely been a beautiful woman at one time...a *really* long time ago. "Oh? Explain."

"I used to work in weapons development." I lied. Well, it wasn't exactly a lie. I really was good at playing around with tech and weapons, making them deadlier and more efficient. "I have some stuff on me that repels the Xathi."

"What kind of weapons would you even have?" the old woman asked.

"How do neuro-grenades that can halt Xathi attacks sound?" I shot back.

There was stunned silence.

"Guaranteed effectiveness," I posited.

Apparently, it had the desired effect

She nodded, then indicated for my cell to be opened. As I walked out of my cell, she smiled at the two of us. "You will escort Dr. Parr to and from the clinic only. You are not to go anywhere else without an escort. Understood?"

I opened my mouth to say something, but Evie elbowed me in the side, then flashed me a look that shut me up.

"Good," Madam Raschke smiled. "Oh, one more thing. The attacks have weakened almost all of our residential structures. Space is at a premium, even using the barracks. You'll have to share, but since you're so close, that won't be a problem, will it?" She laughed as she walked away, her guards following.

Evie and I looked at one another.

I didn't think she was happy with me.

Again.

EVIE

I didn't speak to Sakev the entire walk to the room
provided for me. I didn't want to hear his voice. I
didn't look at him as we walked.I partially blamed
myself.

It was a serious lack of judgment on my part to
think that someone who tried to take on a swarm of
hybrids on their own would be able to act responsibly
in any other situation.

If I'd known he was carrying the neuro-grenades, it
would've made our entrance into Einhiv so much
smoother. City officials would've been begging us to
enter their city, rather than trying to kill us.

But no, Sakev had to keep that little tidbit of
valuable information to himself. As a result, I'd had to

spend valuable time arguing with bureaucrats on his behalf.

The room the city allowed me to use was in one of Einhiv's many barracks set up to house the temporary workers that flooded the city during the harvest seasons. My accommodations were on the second floor, up a rusty staircase bolted to the side of the building. I hadn't been given a key, just a code to punch into the outdated keypad beside the door.

The keypad flashed red, refusing to open the door.

"I'm not in the mood for this," I muttered to no one in particular, even though Sakev was only feet away. I punched the code in once more, only for it to be rejected again.

"You're sure that's the right code?" Sakev peered closely at the keypad.

"Yes, I'm sure," I snapped.

"This keypad is ancient," he muttered. "I bet the wires are completely fried."

"Let's go back to the station and get a new code," I suggested.

"Nonsense," Sakev dismissed me with a wave of his hand. "Watch this." He stepped up to the door and produced two thin lengths of refined scrap metal. With unexpected care and precision, he slipped the metal strips into the crack between the wall and the door.

"Are you serious?" I looked around, making sure no

one could see us. Sakev was already in enough trouble. Anyone would assume he was breaking in, given his track record within the city.

"No, I'm Sakev," he said, deadpan.

"That was terrible. Even for you," I snorted.

He wiggled the metal picks until the door clicked and swung open.

"Piece of cake," he said proudly.

"Should I ask why you know how to do that?" I looked at Sakev out of the side of my eye.

"Probably not." He stepped into the room and looked around. "It's nice." Sakev nodded in appreciation.

He was definitely just being polite. It was a small room with bare walls. Most of the space was occupied by the double bed.

There was roughly a foot of walking space around the perimeter of the bed and one table, completely eclipsed under the lamp it bore, shoved into the corner. Enough for one person, but not two.

"That's your bed." I pointed to the narrow space between the edge of the bed and the wall. At least half of him was going to end up under the bed if he was going to fit. The mental image brought a smug smile to my face.

"You're funny." Sakev threw his pack down on the bed. The action made the walls shudder.

"I'm not joking." I folded my arms across my chest. I was still pissed at him. Everything he did caused more problems for me.

"You're insane if you think I'm sleeping on the floor." Sakev stretched out on the bed, the picture of relaxation.

"Get off!" I fumed. I grabbed his leg and pulled, though it had little effect.

"I was going to thank you for standing up to the officials on my behalf. But now I think I'd be safer in the cell," Sakev chuckled, then his face grew grim.

"I'm truly sorry for killing that man. I would've avoided it if I thought I could. You believe that, don't you?" There was a crack in his good-humored façade, the tiniest glimmer of vulnerability. My opinion mattered to him.

"Of course, I know that." I tugged at my ponytail. "Those jerks started it. You finished it. I appreciate what you did for the clinic and the patients."

"Then what's the problem?"

"The problem is, you're carrying around weapons specifically designed to repel Xathi in an area swarming with Xathi minions and you decided not to say anything." I gestured wildly. Talking with my hands was something I'd directly inherited from my mother, the most dramatic woman who ever lived.

Sakev was trying not to laugh but to his credit, I could see his shoulders shaking.

"I'm sorry," Sakev spoke through his laughter. "I learned a long time ago not to show all my cards at once. But you're just so angry and cute."

"One more condescending word out of you and I'm going to smash your holo-disguise and throw you out!" I was shocked at the words coming out of my mouth. I'd never spoken to anyone like that in my life.

Sakev knew how to get under my skin. He enjoyed it, too.

"It shall be amusing to see you try." The arrogance in his voice was enough to make my blood boil.

"I thought I was doing you a favor by getting you out of that hospital bed," I snapped. "I see now that I should've left you behind.

"You'd be dead by now if I weren't here." Sakev insisted.

I threw my head back and laughed.

"No, I'd be fine. No one here wants to kill me. They want to kill *you*." I jabbed a finger at his chest. He flashed a rakish smile as he grabbed my arm. His grip was firm, but not painful.

This was a sparring match, not a fight.

A dance.

A game.

I fought against him, curious to see what he'd do. He

rolled his eyes and gave my arm a good tug, careful not to hurt me.

I lost my footing as I lurched forward. I fell over him.

"Not so tough now, are you?" I could hear the smirk in his voice.

"Still tougher than you," I snapped. An obvious lie, but I was ready to disagree with him about anything and everything purely out of spite.

"We'll see about that." Before I could blink, Sakev flipped me over and pinned me down. I didn't feel trapped. He kept enough of his weight off me that I could really escape if I wanted to.

But as I thought about it, I realized I didn't want to escape.

My eyes met his.

His gaze was filled with wicked amusement, while mine was surely filled with something like rage, but not quite.

The tether of tension between us snapped.

One moment we were glaring at each other, and the next, I felt his lips crash into mine. My hands wound into his hair, refusing to let him break the kiss. I felt his tongue slide over my teeth. I bit his bottom lip.

I didn't realize my jacket was off until I felt his hand traveling up underneath my shirt. I put my hand against his shoulder and shoved, rolling him off me and climbing on top.

My shirt was removed and his hot hands were roving over my skin. His hands were rough and calloused–the hands of someone who knew hard work.

The explosion of heat and arousal made me feel lightheaded. I looked down at Sakev and frowned. He was gazing up at me, panting slightly, but it wasn't really him.

The tanned skin I was touching wasn't his real skin.

"Get rid of your holo-disguise," I ordered. "I want to see you. The real you."

He looked confused, then surprised, before obliging.

I ran my hands over his chest, pulling his shirt open as I did. He sat up, taking time to kiss my collarbone, shoulders, and breasts and I clawed the shirt off him.

"Funny, you don't seem to have much to complain about now," Sakev growled in my ear. I raked my nails down his back in response. A shudder rippled through his body. "Now you've done it."

He lifted me, rolling me until I was belly down on the bed with my legs dangling off the side.

My legs kicked and I squirmed. I felt the absence of his body in a keen, sharp way. I tried to move backward, to touch his body with mine. His hand met the small of my back, flattened me downward again. My fingers twisted into sheets, covers. I felt nothing but the mattress against my skin but I wanted more—so much more.

I shivered as his fingers ran down my spine, outlining and circling every hard arch of the high bones there.

"You're driving me insane."

"Am I?" His breath, warm and fast, washed across the skin of my shoulder. I gulped and writhed again. The pressure of the bed on my mound, on the hard nub of flesh there, made pleasure zoom into my being.

My toes curled. "You know you are."

His fingers raced along my back cheeks. His nails scratched lightly against that flesh, made my muscles tense. My teeth caught my lower lip and held it. A little shiver stole through my whole body as his fingers traced the cleft between those cheeks, raced out of that crevice and stroked along the slopes of the surrounding flesh.

His breath met the skin on my lower back. I curled upward, my body hunching into a question mark shape against the pillows and mattress.

Words lifted into my throat. I couldn't say them, couldn't give him anymore power over me then he already had. I'd gone weak somehow, and I wanted him.

How to say that?

His fingers dipped between my legs, found the standing ridge of my shivering flesh. His fingers pressed against it, and a low guttural moan broke from my mouth. My teeth snapped at the pillows.

Two fingers of his other hand slid into my wet depths. He kept up the pressure on my clit as he slid his fingers into my body and withdrew them. My inner thighs began to spasm as my core clenched and my breath began a hard and sharp pant. I twisted backward, my whole body shaking as I tried to give him a batter angle of penetration, an easier access to my clit.

My core clenched, fluttered. More juices spilled from inside my body, spilled over his fingers as they entered me again. He moved harder and faster, and my body met that pace. My cries grew louder and longer.

Heat and friction met then snapped. My body went rigid, taut and inflexible as I beat at the pillows.

His fingers raced inside me and then withdrew. He circled my clit and tweaked it, lightly, just enough to bring up a small bit of pain—and a whole lot of pleasure.

The orgasm crashed over me, no holding back, no drawing it out for the sake of prolonging that intense and delicious pleasure. I collapsed onto the bed, limp and shaken. I lifted my head and our mouths met. His was hot and tasted fresh and spicy at the same time. His tongue teased mine. My nipples went stiff and pointed, rising in pebble-hard peaks.

"Still hate me?" Sakev snaked an arm around my shoulders and pulled me up against his chest.

"You're a pain in the ass, but I don't hate you." I curled close to him. His skin was still hot.

"The feeling is mutual." He planted a kiss on the top of my head.

That was the last thing I remembered as I drifted off to sleep.

SAKEV

It was the oddest dream I've ever had, and not one that I wanted to remember. I opened my eyes to see that Evie was already up and dressed.

"Good morning," I yawned. I rolled myself out of the bed, my nakedness on display for Evie to behold.

She didn't even look at me when she answered with a "good morning" of her own. "Get dressed, we have a lot of work to do today." She kept her back to me as she finished prepping her gear. I arched my eyebrows a bit, then shrugged.

Last night happened, I remember.

Skrell, my *body* remembered last night happening. I could see what Vrehx, Axtin, and Tu'ver had seen in their human women...the sweetness, the responsiveness.

There was nothing like it.

Nothing like her.

But for whatever reasons, she didn't walk to talk about it.

With a shrug and a grunt, I grabbed my clothes and dressed myself. I had just slipped on my shirt when she finally turned to look at me. "Evie," I acknowledged as I sat down and pulled on my boots.

"Sakev," she said back with a nod. "We've got a lot of things to do at the clinic, can you behave today?"

I put on the most innocent look I could manage. "Of course!" I affirmed with enthusiasm. She laughed and threw a rag at me. I ducked to the side and laughed along with her. At least she wasn't angry with me. That was good.

"Finish putting on your big-ass boots, and let's get to work," she snapped playfully as she walked out the door. I grabbed my own gear (again, better to be prepared at all times,) snapped on the disguise and followed her out the door, along the hall, and down the stairs.

She set such a quick pace that I had to take the steps two at a time in order to keep up, and I didn't catch her until we reached the bottom.

"Slow down. They'll still be there," I said as I came up next to her.

"Speed up, slowpoke." Her smile was phenomenal.

"You didn't mind my apparent lack of speed last night," I quipped, matching her smile.

Her smile faded a bit, replaced by a little embarrassment. "Yeah, let's not talk about that while we're working," she said.

It was a few steps before she added, "Don't want to distract you. You seem to need to concentrate 'hard' to finish things."

I was wounded.

She had plunged a knife into my maleness. It was painful. I stopped dead as she kept walking. She eventually stopped, looked back, and motioned for me to catch up with a twitch of her head.

The smile on her face let me in on the joke.

I gave a playful growl as I jogged up to her, and we walked to the clinic, with not a care in the world as we laughed along the way. Back at the clinic, Evie got straight to work. She looked in on the people still wounded from yesterday's attack, double-checking their bandages and write-ups. She did an ultrasound on a pregnant woman, explaining to me what she was doing while she did it.

As odd as it all was, I found myself interested. Or, was I just interested in her? I wasn't sure. But it didn't matter.

Evie was in her element, and it was fun to see.

Then one of the guards came in, a nasty scrape to his jaw. He explained that someone had accosted him, knocking him to the ground, before running away. I looked back at the three guards that had been assigned to us and motioned them over.

"Are you allowed to talk to me about the city's defenses and weaponry?"

One of the guards, a medium-built man with dark skin, nodded. "Yes, sir. Madam Raschke has explained that you are willing to help us against the Xathi, and that we are to give you whatever information we deem pertinent to your needs."

Very big words. "Very well." I looked back at Evie. "Evie?"

"What?"

"Are you using this table right here?"

"Does it look like I'm using that table?" While the words sounded mean, her tone of voice was playful, so I answered back accordingly.

"Well, not right now, but I was wondering if you were thinking of throwing me on it later to work off some stress."

"Sakev, if I could throw you right now, it wouldn't be on a table," she replied, giving me a glare as a signal to quit the line of conversation.

The guards looked at us like we were out of our minds.

We probably were.

Our gazes lingered and I saw her break into a smile.

She shook her head and let us use the table as she went back to looking at reports and mixing together medicine to help with her patients.

I grabbed a nearby tablet while I directed the guards to move the table to the far side of the room.

I handed the guard that had spoken to me the datapad. "Show me an overhead view of the city," I asked as he tapped on the screen, then handed it back to me.

"I don't know your name."

"I'm Sakev," I volunteered. If I was going to be working with him, I might as well know these human's names.

"I'm Tona," the dark-skinned guard replied. "This is Nathan, and this is Skit," he indicated the other two. Nathan was a big man, almost as tall as me, but not nearly in the same shape. He had a bit of a pudge in his middle section. Skit was small, just an inch or two taller than Evie. Both nodded as I acknowledged them.

"Very well." I toyed around with the picture of the city a bit, highlighting all the defensive locations that I saw, as well as the weak points that I noticed. "Tell me about what you have."

Skit pointed at the defensive locations I had marked. "Each of those is an entry point into the city, blocked by a gate, which is guarded by anywhere from five to seven guards at a time. Three fully-automated turrets, two rocket launchers, and several hundred rounds located at every gate."

"I noticed the towers you have spread around the town are separate from the gates. Why is that?"

Again, Skit was the one to answer. Nathan and Tona seemed more than willing to let him handle the conversation. "It was done to ensure that a warning would be given to the denizens of the city in the event of an attack. If the tower was attacked, the people at the gate could then alert the town and vice versa."

I gave an appreciative nod. That was smart. "Tell me about the tower defenses."

"Each tower is outfitted with a fully-automatic, medium-range blaster and a rocket launcher. The guards assigned to the towers are also equipped with long-range blaster rifles."

"Good. Good," I pointed to the marks that I had made in yellow. "Do you see these points here?" At their nods, I continued. "These are weak points in your defenses. You have the towers and gates well-positioned to see *most* of your weak points in the wall, but there are a few spots you missed."

We spent the next two hours talking about how to strengthen the weak points and how to get a better guard rotation established, as well as potential escape routes and procedures in case the Xathi did come and prove too much for them.

Skit was good. He had a real mind for military tactics. It was a shame that he was wasted as a simple guard in a town like this. I considered asking if he wanted to come back to the *Vengeance* with us when we returned, but since my disguise was still active, I wasn't sure how he would react to me and the others.

That's when I decided to broach the next subject. "Can you talk to me about that group that attacked us yesterday?"

This was where Tona took over the conversation, while Nathan looked away. "They...they are an... interesting group, to say the least."

"That would be an understatement," I replied.

To which, Tona cleared his throat before continuing, "They're what's left of our attempt to form into a resistance army. When those ships came crashing into the planet and all those creatures showed up, we tried to come together. There just wasn't enough of us willing to be a full-time army and do what an army was supposed to do to keep it all together. The ones who kept at it became their own group."

At his pause, I looked at them. Skit was still studying the datapad, while Nathan stared at me. He looked uncomfortable, and that made me uncomfortable. Tona kept going. "They're led, if you can really use that word, by a young man named Bastien. He and his family had been in Nyheim on business when the ship crashed. He came back, but his family didn't. He's been leading the anti-alien charge ever since."

"Maybe I could talk to him, see what his ideas are about fighting the Xathi," I suggested.

Tona shook his head. "That wouldn't be a good idea. He's not exactly all there, if you know what I mean. He blames all the aliens for his family being dead, not just the Xathi. He says that the Skotans, K'ver, and whatever that other race is are all responsible and that they all need to pay."

I nodded, trying to look sympathetic. I was a bit concerned about Tona's words though. "So, he knows what the other aliens are?"

"Yeah. He tells everyone who's willing to listen, and even those who aren't, that we need to keep our eyes out for them all. He explained that Skotans have scales like a lizard, K'ver have tech built into their skin, and all the other ones...I can't remember their names...but that they're berserkers who love to fight. He said they're all dangerous, and that they need to be eliminated."

This information worried me. How did this Bastien character know so much about us? Yes, we'd been around humans, but could the information have traveled here that quickly? Something wasn't right. There was something not right at all.

And why did Nathan keep staring at me like that?

EVIE

I felt good.

Really good.

Sakev might be more trouble than he's worth, but he was damn good at stress relief. Not a bad pillow, either, now that I had a chance to think on it. I hadn't gotten such a good night's sleep since before the Xathi attacked Fraga.

I wasn't sure where Sakev had wandered off to, but he promised he would be on his best behavior. It was time I gave him some credit and trusted him a little more. He'd gotten me into a lot of trouble since we'd arrived, but he'd also gotten me out of trouble, too.

I struggled to focus on my patients. So far, I'd had nothing unusual. Superficial scrapes, mild cases of the sniffles, and an occasional allergic reaction. I could handle everything on autopilot. But the moment I let my mind wander to Sakev and the night before, it didn't take much for my face to flush with color.

That Skotan moron had me hot and bothered. He was nice to look at, and he was actually funny.

Sure, he took great pleasure in pushing my buttons.

But I liked to push his, too.

Literally and figuratively, as it turned out.

I was still daydreaming about Sakev when a young woman walked up to me. She was small, shorter than me even. Her thick, unruly hair was chopped off at chin-length. Her nose and cheeks were smattered with freckles, which only drew attention to the biggest eyes I'd ever seen. She looked like a lost doe, sweet and fragile.

"Hi, honey, what can I do for you?" I asked gently. Something about her made me want to speak that way. I rarely called patients pet names, but she looked so uncomfortable. I couldn't blame her. She'd probably heard about the anti-alien group coming in and trying to trash the place.

"Can you help with headaches?" she asked in a small voice.

"Absolutely," I assured her. "How long have you had them?"

"I rarely got them before. But I've had one almost every single day for the past two weeks." I ushered her to one of the examination areas and drew the curtain around us. She eased herself onto the examination table.

"Have you tried any medication?" I passed her a datapad, so she could enter her personal information.

"Everything I could get my hands on." She finished and passed the datapad back to me. I pulled up her records.

Marigold Harris. If I remembered correctly, a marigold was a beautiful flower that grew on Old Earth. It was unusual to come across someone with a name like that.

I was surprised to see she was almost nineteen years old. Her frame was so slight, and she had such a quiet way about her that I'd assumed she was younger.

"And nothing worked?" I prompted. She shook her head.

"Nothing made a difference. I'd never felt a headache like this before. I tried to see a doctor sooner, but everyone who might've been able to help me went to help people in other cities," she explained.

"Well, I'll do everything I can to help you while I'm here." I smiled as I grabbed some examination tools. "Let me check your vitals, and then we'll get into solving this headache problem."

Marigold smiled. When I moved behind her to listen to her heart and lungs, I noticed something odd. There were pale, somewhat iridescent patches of skin at the base of her neck.

"Marigold, what are these patches here on your skin?" I kept my voice steady. The last thing I wanted was to raise alarm.

"What patches?" She asked, turning her head. I held up a mirror so she could see them. "I didn't even know I had those." She looked nervous.

A stone of dread settled in my stomach. Of course, I didn't know anything for a fact yet. Perhaps this was just an unusual skin condition. But I had to acknowledge the possibility that I was looking at the early stages of whatever caused hybridism.

"If it's okay, I'd like to run more tests."

"Yeah, that's okay." I didn't miss the nervousness in her voice.

"I'm going to have to put you in a room by yourself, just in case it's contagious," I explained. "You'll be able to call me if you need something. It's just a precaution, okay?"

She nodded slowly. I escorted her to an empty observation room, and asked a clinic volunteer to fetch water and a few books for Marigold.

"If you feel anything, I want you to press this button," I gave her a small square device with a large white button. "I'll get a message and come right to you."

"Okay," she said, voice wavering.

"I'll be back as soon as I can," I assured her. "I just want to see if anyone else has similar symptoms to you. I can test you all at once, and we can get to the bottom of this all the more quickly."

"Okay," she repeated.

I gave her a bright smile as I left. I really hoped this was nothing.

Back in the lobby, I asked for anyone experiencing unusual, persistent headaches to come see me immediately. Twelve people of varying ages and genders stood and walked toward me. One by one, I took them into the examination area.

Out of the twelve I examined, three had similar patches on their skin like Marigold's. A man in his late sixties, a woman in her early forties, and a man who worked as a city official, but had taken a sick day. I ushered them to the quarantine area prattling on about how they were going to help me solve a mystery.

Marigold looked relieved when I brought the others in.

I questioned them separately. I started with easy questions. *Do the patches itch? Have you noticed them anywhere else on your body?* I worked up to the more difficult questions afterward.

"Has anything changed in your mental state lately?" A long shot, a gamble. But I held my breath while they thought about it.

"I didn't think anything of it at first," the other woman, Xella, confessed. "It didn't seem unusual during the moment. I can't explain it. But, to answer your question, yes."

"I hear noises that don't make sense with my surroundings," the official, Dyn, told me. "Like, I'll be on patrol in an urban area, but I'll hear the sound of rain or intense wind that isn't there. I figured it was just part of these crazy headaches."

Marigold confessed she heard a woman's voice whenever she was trying to sleep. She figured it was her overactive imagination.

The old man, Rolf, swore he heard his late wife calling his name on multiple occasions.

All of them had trouble sleeping at night.

"I'd like to run a few more tests," I announced to my quarantine patients. All of them looked uneasy. I didn't know how to comfort them. I wanted to tell them everything was fine, that they shouldn't worry. But there was a chance I'd be lying to them, which I'd never do. With what I hoped was a reassuring smile, I left the room.

Once outside I paused.

Should I lock it? If they weren't infected, if this was just some unknown illness that had nothing to do with the hybrids, with the Xathi, would this be a betrayal of my patients?

But if it was…

Heart in my throat, I locked the door.

Just to keep other folks from risking infection. That was all, really.

The clinic had a small lab, run by the surviving med students, that was able to handle basic tests.

"Do you have any organic material from the hybrids beyond the wall?" I asked a technician, a wiry young man in his early twenties.

"I don't know anyone insane enough to try to harvest samples from those things," he shuddered. "Why?"

"Just curious," I said quickly. I didn't want to cause a panic. "If I brought you an unknown sample, could you identify it?"

"It depends," he shrugged. "We don't have access to the most sophisticated equipment, but the tests we can run are quite fast. It's worth a shot, if you ask me."

"Excellent, I'll have samples sent over soon." It wasn't the best, but at least I could make some progress. "I don't suppose I could run a full body resonance scan on a patient, either?"

"Nope." He frowned. He was as frustrated by this as I was. "I do have pod scanners, though."

I'd never worked with pod scanners. They were designed for field use when a proper hospital wasn't an option. The scanner could fit in the palm of my hand.

The images they produced weren't detailed, but they were enough to discern if something was abnormal.

They'd have to do.

I pocketed a few of the scanners and returned to the quarantine room.

"I'm going to do a simple brain scan. Don't worry, it won't hurt a bit."

The pod scanners were easy to use. It took only moments to scan everyone. Afterward, I carefully scraped a small sample of the abnormal skin patches and prepped them for testing.

"Do you know what's wrong with us?" Marigold asked before I could leave the room.

"Not yet, but I'm getting close," I said brightly. I hurried back to the lab, feeling more uneasy with each passing moment. I certainly was close to finding an answer, I just doubted it would be a happy one.

"Here are the samples I need tested." I passed the skin samples to the technician before pulling up the images from the pod scanner. The images weren't as detailed as I would've liked, but I was able to make out some concerning similarities among them.

All of their brain activity scans showed patterns similar to those of schizophrenics. Even more concerning was a pitch-black patch at the base of their brains.

I had theories of what it could be, but I couldn't

determine anything for sure with the testing methods available to me.

I ran back to the quarantine area and examined the base of their skulls. Sure enough, I felt something solid on each of them.

The signs were pointing to early stages of hybridism. But I needed to know more. Perhaps there was a way to reverse it before it got worse.

I needed to know what that mass was at the base of their skulls.

Without more information, I didn't know how I was going to help them.

SAKEV

Our room was empty when I got back.

A split second of panic set in before I remembered that Tona, Skit, and Nathan were watching Evie. As much as I didn't really trust anyone here, I also knew they would keep her safe.

That, and I doubted Bastien's crew of "alien haters" would dare another attack right now. The regular people were too on edge, and the guards were roaming around everywhere.

My stomach growled, but I ignored it. Something bothered me about my conversation with the guards. I had asked them how they thought Bastien knew about the aliens, obviously without revealing my true identity, and why he thought the others were so dangerous.

That's when Nathan finally broke his silence.

He told me that *no*, no one had ever seen an alien in Einhiv, not since that first "crystal bug-thing" had arrived a few days after the ships had crashed. Since then, no one had seen an alien. That was when they had decided to build the walls, using construction equipment and materials originally intended for a new settlement on the northern coast.

So, if Einhiv had never seen any of us, from what they told me, then how did Bastien know about us?

We weren't in Nyheim after the crash, and when we did go there, it had been to help Axtin save Leena. We never made it into the actual city itself, or at least, the city that was still standing.

I thought about how many people died in that crash, and how many more didn't get a chance to escape before the Xathi captured them for food or turned them into monsters.

I lay back on the bed, my arm under my head. It made no sense to me. How could Bastien have that kind of information? Nothing made sense as I started dozing off. I woke up, my free hand on my knife, as the door opened. In walked Evie, carrying three bags and a vase with flowers.

"You got me flowers," I acknowledged, teasing her. "I have to admit, they're not really my style. I prefer those red and purple ones that try to eat me whenever I go outside," I joked as she closed the door.

She laughed as she walked to the single window in the room. She placed the flowers on the windowsill and turned to me. "They're to make the room seem a little more...homier. If I have to look at your ugly face all night, I figured I'd bring something pretty into the room."

I put my hand over my heart and faked a gasp. "Ah! The pain, the wounding. Here, take the knife from my heart, and bury it in my skull so I can't feel the pain anymore."

I pantomimed pulling a knife out and held my hand out to her. She "grabbed" the fake knife and "plunged" it back into my body several times. We laughed as she placed the bags down next to the bed.

That's when I finally paid attention to my nostrils and the amazing smell emanating from the bags.

"What is that delectable smell?"

"Food, stupid," she laughed as she began pulling out container after container of food. "One thing they have an over-abundance of here. At the end of the day, I think every patient I saw today brought a dish as a thank-you. Even with sending half of it home with the students, it's a lot."

She looked around, a bit lost, then shrugged as I sat up on the bed. "Looks like we're eating up here," she said as she started putting food on the bed itself.

I didn't argue. My stomach rumbled and grumbled as she pulled more and more food out of the bags.

"By everything that is holy and imagined! How much food did you bring?" I asked as she put yet another container on the bed. There was nearly no room left for us to sit.

She laughed as she took out the final two containers and tossed the bags into the corner. "Don't be so overdramatic. We did this all the time when I was growing up."

"Did what?" I asked as I unpacked the plates and utensils she had brought.

"*This*," she said, with a wave of her hand. She sat down on the bed across from me, the food between us. "Growing up, for special occasions, my family used to get a bunch of food, and we'd sit around on the floor, just eating whatever we could grab. We would talk, watch whatever entertainment we could find, and just enjoy each other's company."

And that's exactly what Evie and I proceeded to do.

We spent the next few minutes picking through the food, piling it onto our plates, and mumbling about what we had done during the day.

"You know," I started as I ladled on my second helping of long starchy strands mixed with vegetables and meat. "I don't think I've ever done anything so..." I struggled to find the word.

"So what?" she asked, grabbing one of the fried morsels of diced vegetables in batter. Those tasted good, too.

"So...domesticated."

She tilted her head a bit to the side as she looked at me. "What do you mean 'domesticated'? You've never eaten with family before?"

"No. Not really." I took an oversized bite of what she called *lo mein*, relishing the taste of it.

"You mean, you've never sat down with family, and just bullshitted over dinner?"

"No."

"Why not?"

"I'd rather not talk about it, honestly." I wasn't in a particularly good mood anymore. The food had lost a bit of the taste.

She pushed a fried food roll towards me.

I nodded my thanks, put the roll on my plate, and got another portion from the plate of grilled meat. I didn't answer her, and just focused on eating.

She took the hint and changed the subject. "There was this one time, when I was maybe six or seven, and we were eating. My dad was trying to tell us a very animated story, using his fork to mimic something. I can't even remember what it was exactly." She started laughing a bit in remembrance. "He got a little too exuberant and ended up poking my mother in the head with the fork, getting it stuck in her hair. I don't think we had ever laughed that hard before."

She told me more stories of her family and the meals they had, the vacations. I told her a bit of my life growing up, the parts that I could tell her.

My family dynamic was much different compared to hers.

It was late, and I struggled to hold in a yawn.

"Wimp!" she laughed as she pointed at me.

"What?"

"You yawned first. That means you're tired, and that means you're a wimp. It was a game my siblings and I played when we were little." Then she yawned.

My eyebrows raised, my mouth dropped, and I pointed at her.

"What?" she asked. "I'm allowed to yawn now. You yawned first, so you broke the rules." She stuck her tongue out at me and started clearing the food off the bed.

I helped her clear, then we both began to change.

After, we sat back down on the bed. "So, I learned some interesting news today about our attackers," I announced, looking at her.

She turned to me, an eyebrow raised. "Oh?"

I told her about what Tona, Skit, and Nathan had told me about Bastien. I also told her about my suspicions about Bastien's knowledge of us.

"It makes no sense how he knows about you. Not *you*, you, but all of you." She sat on the bed in silence for a few minutes, as did I. "What if Bastien is hiding information?"

"What do you mean?" I asked.

"Well, the others have shown themselves to other humans, ones that have travelled to other towns. What if one of them talked to Bastien? Could any of the refugees have come here? Or maybe Bastien travelled out of town and saw you guys?"

It made sense. I had been thinking it, but hearing her mirror my thoughts made me feel more confident about my ideas. She yawned again, which made me yawn, too. She laughed, saying something about not being able to fight it, but it was muffled by another yawn of her own.

We both laughed and decided to lie down.

We fought, playfully, about who got to sleep against the wall.

"If someone breaks in and shoots at us, you'll block the shots," she said, trying to sound serious.

I gave credence to it. Because it was the same as my argument, she just said it first.

"Very well. I'll protect you from intruders," I conceded. "Just remember, if I roll over and fall out of bed, I might drag you down with me," I said with a wink.

Her eyes twinkled as she slowly agreed, "I'll just take my chances."

Our bodies melded together as we settled in the bed.

She moved around until she was comfortable, her back towards mine, and said, "Good night." I did my best to get comfortable, which wasn't hard, considering my past. I had spent many a night sleeping in some strange places. I had learned to be comfortable in uncomfortable places.

After nearly an hour, her breathing was regular, but I was still awake. What the guards had told me still weighed on my mind. Evie's explanation that Bastien had talked to other refugees, or had seen us personally, made sense, but it seemed too easy. Could that be all there was? There was just something wrong with the whole thing.

I felt her shiver a bit as she slept, so I slowly and gently wrapped my arms around her. Our combined body heat stopped her shivering, and I was finally comfortable enough to fall asleep.

EVIE

I entered the clinic feeling refreshed and optimistic. It'd been so long since I'd spent an evening like that.

The last time my family was together in one place was years ago. There was an Old Earth holiday called Thanksgiving that we liked to celebrate just because it gave us an excuse to see each other, and to eat way more than we should.

None of us knew the particulars of Thanksgiving. We knew there were specific dishes that were usually served, but we didn't know what they were. There was also a specific date to celebrate, but the likelihood of all of us being available on that day was slim. So, we got together whenever we could, ate a bunch, and slapped a fancy name on the day to make it extra special.

I could hardly believe I'd told Sakev so much about my family. I hadn't mentioned them once since I boarded the *Vengeance*. I tried not to think about them. But sitting on the bed with all that food brought back so many wonderful memories.

I'd been unable to contact my family since the Xathi attacked Fraga. My parents lived in Glymna. As far as I knew, the Xathi had yet to reach that city. Both of my sisters lived in small towns outside bigger cities. The Xathi prioritized attacking and harvesting big cities, but with the hybrid hoards popping up everywhere, I didn't know if my sisters were safe or not.

I'm sure my family thought I was dead. I wished I had a way to contact them. But, for right now, focusing on the happy memories was enough. We'd find each other again when this was over.

My optimistic mood vanished the moment I entered the clinic. Anya, one of the volunteers, a young woman with perpetual dark circles under her eyes, ran up to me.

"You've got to come quick," she shrieked. I tried to calm her. I didn't want the waiting patients to overhear and become nervous. "There's something happening in quarantine." She had the good sense to whisper that part, though her voice was shaking. I followed her at a run toward the quarantine area. Nothing could've prepared me for what I saw.

Overnight, the crystal patches had spread across their skin. Their whole bodies were covered now. Two of them had even sprouted crystalline shards on their forearms. They were animalistic, circling and lunging at each other, snapping with teeth that had grown into points.

"We need to separate them," I ordered.

"How?" Anya asked. "No one's willing to go in there." She was right. Entering the quarantine room would be disastrous. I couldn't risk anyone else becoming infected.

Marigold noticed us standing outside the observation window. She let out a horrible, inhuman screech before hurling herself at the wall. Anya and I flinched, hurrying backward. The walls and windows were reinforced, but not indestructible. Eventually, Marigold and the others would break through.

"Go find Sakev." He was the only one who'd had personal experience with the hybrids. He might know what to do. "I think he's with the officials in the lobby." Anya looked relieved at something to do as she fled the room. I wouldn't be surprised if she didn't come back.

There was an intercom mounted on the wall inside the quarantine room. I pressed the button, but I wasn't sure what to say. Would they understand me? Rolf, the older man, leaped at Xella. Their crystalized skin crunched as it made contact with the linoleum floors.

"Enough!" I shouted into the intercom. They all paused for a moment, looking around wildly for the source of the sound. "Marigold, can you understand me?" Marigold had no reaction to her name being called.

She didn't know it was hers anymore.

"Can any of you understand me?" I asked, growing more desperate. The sound of my voice coming through the speakers agitated them. I was surprised they couldn't locate the source.

When I'd spoken with Sakev back in the med bay on the *Vengeance,* he'd told me the hybrids were capable of coordinating an ambush. The four before me looked like they were only capable of the most primal behaviors.

Hopefully, Sakev could give me some insight.

I was relieved when he showed up.

I wasn't surprised that Anya wasn't with him. If I had a choice, I wouldn't be here either.

"What's going on?" His brow furrowed with worry.

"Look at them." I gestured to the quarantine area. "This happened overnight. I didn't know hybridism could take hold so quickly."

Sakev's expression hardened as he took in the sight of the quarantine patients. When he didn't say anything, I spoke again.

"You know more about hybrids than anyone here. I

don't know what to do." I half-expected Sakev to make a show of me begging for help, and to crack a joke or two. I would've felt better if he had. The hard look on his face was unnerving.

"I know what to do." Without looking at me, he strode to the door. He entered, before I could tell him not to. I ran to the intercom and pressed the button.

"What the hell do you think you're doing?" I shouted. The quarantine patients were circling him, unsure of what to do about the intruder. "Get out of there right now, Sakev!"

He pulled out his blaster. My stomach sank as I realized what his solution was.

"Don't!" I shouted.

It was too late.

He fired four shots, each one hitting its target square in the center of the forehead. They dropped to the floor, motionless. It was over in seconds. Sakev tucked his blaster back into its holster and exited the room.

"Why would you do that?" Tears stung my eyes as my vision blurred. I tried to blink the tears away, but one escaped and rolled down my cheek. I didn't know what angered me more — the dead patients or Sakev's calm demeanor.

"It was the only thing that could be done," was Sakev's only explanation as he walked through the

door, leaving me alone with the bodies in the next
room.

I wanted to scream and break anything I could get
my hands on. How could Sakev say something like
that? I clamped a hand over my mouth so I wouldn't
cry.

"I heard a noise—oh my God!" Anya had entered the
room. The color drained from her face as she took in
the bodies. "He shot them?"

"He said it was the only thing that can be done," my
voice wavered, but I knew he was right.

I didn't have enough information to know how the
infection spread, much less any idea how to reverse it.

And the people, now hybrids, would have killed
anyone they could.

Sakev had made that cold calculation instantly and
done the only thing possible. But it scared me.

This wasn't the world I wanted to live in.

I was glad someone else was there now. Being in the
presence of another person forced me to pull myself
together.

I might not like it, but this was our reality now.
Time to deal.

"What should we do?" Anya was still staring at them.

"We can't bring them back." I dabbed at my eyes.
"But we can still learn from them. Is the morgue in
operation?"

"No, but I'm sure we can come up with something."
Anya moved closer to the door, eager to leave.

I decided to give her a break.

"Go see what kind of accommodations can be made.
I'll stay here and see what I can find out." Anya left with
a grateful nod.

I located a mask and a pair of gloves to cover my
mouth and nose. I still didn't know how hybridism
spread, but I felt better going in with some degree of
protection.

Marigold was closest to the door. I knelt beside her,
gingerly rotating her head. Her eyes were still open.
Though Sakev's shot had been effective, the
crystallization of her skin had kept damage to a
minimum.

From here, I could see the crystal coat was
approximately a quarter of an inch thick. Each strand
of her hair was also coated in a thin layer of crystal. I
couldn't believe how fast it'd consumed her.

I ran my hand over her hair. It was rough and stiff.

"I'm so sorry this happened to you," I whispered. "It
just happened so fast."

She was so young. The records said her birthday
was next month. She would've been nineteen.

Tears welled in my eyes again, but I held them back.
I couldn't let the mask on my face get wet.

I shifted her head again, so that her neck was

exposed to me. Over the area where I found the solid mass, the crystalline coating was almost a full inch thick. The crystal growths weren't just alarmingly quick, but deliberate as well.

Self-consciously, I reached for the base of my own neck and pressed. Nothing out of the ordinary. I shook my head at myself. I needed to keep it together.

I checked the others and found that the growth patterns of the crystals were the same as Marigold's. The hard mass concealed beneath was clearly significant to the process of becoming a hybrid. I didn't like to admit it, but Sakev may have provided a way to get answers.

I was too emotionally invested in this, that was the problem. I'd been scolded for it before, when I worked in a normal hospital on normal patients.

My supervisor at the hospital in Fraga was a stone-cold woman hardened by years of tragic cases. She was damn good at what she did and often told me I could one day be at the top of my field if I stopped letting my emotions get in the way of making rational decisions.

But that wasn't what I wanted.

I cared about Marigold and the others. I still cared about them even though they weren't human in the end. Because I cared, I knew I nothing would stop me from finding answers. Their deaths were going to mean something.

I needed to clear my head. I wouldn't apologize for my emotions, but I needed to calm down before I began examinations.

I left Marigold and the others behind. I hurried through the clinic lobby, not stopping even though people called my name.

I was glad I didn't run into Sakev. I understood his decision, but I was still angry, bewildered.

Maybe, somehow, we could have found another way.

It hadn't been his choice to make.

I left the clinic, stepping into the fresh air.

I kept walking.

SAKEV

I had no idea why Evie was so angry with me.

What I did was necessary, plain and simple.

Those refugees were beyond help. There was nothing left of them. Their humanity was gone, their sanity was gone, the only thing left of them was pure animalistic rage and chaos.

I couldn't let her, or anyone else, for that matter, walk into that room and deal with them.

I *had* to kill them.

Why couldn't she see that?

What was it about Evie that she had such a problem with my action?

It made no sense to me.

I needed to walk, to clear my head, but I had

nowhere to go. I still wasn't allowed outside by myself, so I walked around inside the clinic building.

I tried smiling at people, but several of them still gave me a wide berth, still scared because of the fight a few days ago. It didn't seem to matter what I did, it was wrong.

I shook my head in exasperation and found a stairwell. I figured there would be fewer people on the upper floors of the building, since Evie was the only one able to do actual medical work. She had some nurses around to help, but she was the only one qualified to do any healing until Einhiv's doctor was back on his feet.

At the fourth floor, I stepped out of the stairwell and found myself alone. That was a good thing. I knew that the people were wary of me because of what had happened before, and because of my size.

There weren't very many humans built to my specifications, so it made sense that people would be intimidated.

It was just sad that all they saw was my size, and not me. Of course, if they saw the real me, guaranteed, they'd be even more scared.

My size had served me well before the Xathi.

At first, it was my lack of size that had benefitted me. My mother had never been the most nurturing parent and she forced my siblings and me to work from a young age.

She said that with our father gone, we had to pull our own weight, and that if we couldn't, we had better figure out a way. Since I was the smallest, I had always been tasked with cleaning or sneaking into the smaller spaces.

I was also given the smallest share of anything, whether it was food, a place to sleep, or clothes.

When I had failed to 'acquire' my target too many times, my mother told me that I was no longer welcome in the family and exiled me.

I ended up close to death before I was found...by the most powerful criminal in town. He took me in, fed me, raised me, and trained me. It may not have been the best life in the world, but I was alive, and people seemed to care about me.

My small size was still used to sneak into places, though my rewards were much larger, and my failures were forgiven, as long as I succeeded the next time.

As the years went by, I grew. I went from being the shortest person around to one of the tallest. My boss figured that if I was going to be that tall, I might as well add on the muscle as well.

Thus, I began a whole new life.

I worked out and trained. I learned how to fight. I

lifted weights. I gained the trust of the boss. I gained a reputation, and a bit of a following. The boss eventually called on me for all his major jobs, and those only added to my reputation. People were scared of me. Terrified, even. There weren't many places around town I wasn't able to go. Even the local authorities were afraid of me.

When the boss wanted to expand, I was the one he sent out to make the expansion happen. It was said that my hands were red because of the blood I spilled, not by nature. I looked down at my hands and thought about the people who had died at my hands, and about the things stolen or broken by them. Back then, I didn't care.

I had power. I had respect. I had control.

The boss was the only one bigger than me, and that was only because people respected me and my loyalty to him. My life, while illegal, was worth something.

I was worth something.

When the boss had been injured and laid up, I'd run the show. Things had been going well, and I used my size over others' to keep them going well.

Then, the Xathi attacked.

Everything we had built, everything we had done, was gone.

My first fight with a Xathi had nearly ended me. My size hadn't mattered anymore. They were bigger than me. Faster. The only thing that had saved my life that day was sheer luck.

I joined the military the next day. I had figured that my...background...would work in our fight against the Xathi. I was right, but not the way I had thought. I had never imagined we would fall through a rift in space and end up on a new planet, with new people.

The idea that we would become friends, even lovers, with some of these new people had never crossed my mind either. But then, here we were, and here I was.

Too damaged for Evie.

Yes, I made her smile, I made her laugh, but when I shot those people, she looked at me like I was a monster.

I hadn't meant to hurt her, and I honestly didn't like shooting those poor humans, but there was nothing I could have done. There was nothing anyone could have done.

They were gone.

There had been nothing left of their former selves. What was I supposed to have done? There was no way I could have left them alive, they might have hurt Evie... or someone else. What if they had broken out? What if they had been infectious? I had to kill them. It was the only thing I could do to keep everyone safe.

I looked up and found that I had ended up near a window. It had been broken and the breeze that came through it was nice. Evie would have liked the breeze, and the quiet. I wondered how I was going to fix things, because I didn't want to ever have her look at me like that again.

Then I heard a scream. It had come from outside. Another scream reached my ears, and I knew, in that moment, Evie was in trouble. I ran for the stairwell and cursed my idiotic decision to leave her alone. I practically flew down the stairs to the ground floor. The door to the stairwell barely stayed on its hinges as I crashed through it. I noticed the looks and shouts, but I ignored them all as I rushed down the hall for the building entrance. Evie was in trouble, and it was my fault.

I intended to hurt whatever, or whoever, had gone after her.

EVIE

They didn't react to my screams.

They didn't even flinch. It was like I'd done nothing at all, even though that scream had been loud enough to rattle the windows.

I just hoped someone heard it. I didn't think I was that far from the clinic, but I hadn't been paying attention.

I couldn't believe I'd been so lost in thought that I'd let the group of strangers get this close in the first place.

In my mind, Sakev already scolded me for it.

One of the attackers was close enough to grab my arm.

I yanked away from his grip, stumbling backward,

and slamming into the brick wall of the building behind me.

There were half a dozen men, all carrying crude weapons like lead pipes and bricks, just like the men who had attacked the clinic. As radical as their reputation was, it was odd that they didn't carry proper weapons.

"That's her, Bastien," one of them spoke up. Their pattern of speech was unusual. There was no fluidity.

He spoke like he processed each word separately.

And Bastien? I *knew* that name. Sakev had mentioned it when the anti-alien groups came up. He was their leader, but I didn't know anything else about them.

"That's her alright, Bastien," another one echoed.

"That's her." Odd. The repetitive speech was strange on its own, but they all repeated the phrase with the same tone and pitch. They approached me on all sides, effectively cutting off any means of escape.

"What do you want?" I demanded.

"Alien whore." The man I assumed was Bastien spat at my feet.

"Alien whore."

"Alien whore."

"Alien whore."

The repetition was deeply unsettling. Some of them twitched their heads when they spoke. Jutting their chins at unnatural angles. When they moved, their legs were stiff.

What the hell was going on?

"You're mistaken," I said calmly. "There are no aliens here. I'm a doctor."

"Liar!" Bastien roared. His dark hair was about a week overdue for a haircut. Pieces of it fell forward into his eyes, and it stuck up in the back, making him look even more unstable.

Stranger still, he was wearing a long-sleeved shirt and long pants. The fabric looked thick and sturdy.

Everyone else in the group wore similar attire. It was a hot, humid day.

I was wearing a short-sleeved top and was already feeling too warm. They couldn't have been comfortable, yet none of them looked like they were sweating.

Something definitely wasn't right.

"They're everywhere and must be exterminated." Bastien took a stiff step toward me.

"Exterminated."

"Exterminated."

"Take one more step, and I'll knock your teeth out," I bluffed. Despite the best efforts of my brothers, I didn't know how to throw a good punch, let alone hit someone hard enough to do that, but it seemed like something Sakev would say, and people certainly gave him a wide berth. Though, he was also a giant.

An *armed* giant, at that.

Bastien's laugh was unnatural, like he wasn't sure how to laugh properly. His eyes looked...*off*. Glazed, yet still sharp. His gaze was penetrating, but it was like he was looking right through me. I didn't dare take my eyes off him, but I suspected the others had the same look in their eyes, too.

"What should we do with her?" Bastien asked the others.

"Do with her."

"Do with her."

"Stop that!" I shrieked. The hair on my arms and on the back of my neck had stood up. Something was deeply, deeply wrong with them.

"If you're sick, I can help you." It was a pathetic attempt.

I didn't expect them to lower their pipes and bricks and skip off to the clinic with me.

The movement ticks and the speech repetition pointed to something neurological. I wished I had a pod scanner on me.

"Evie!" It was Sakev. He must have heard me scream. I could've collapsed with relief. It took the group an extra beat to react to him, but when they did, they all turned their heads at the same time. Like they shared a brain.

Like the Xathi.

"Alien scum!" Bastien howled.

"*Alien scum!*"

"*Alien scum!*"

"Evie, would you care to explain this?" Sakev called to me as the men rushed him.

"It's another anti-alien group!"

I looked around for some way to help. There was a palm-sized stone at my feet. I picked it up and hurled it at the group, striking Bastien in the back of the skull. He didn't react at all.

"I figured that out for myself." Sakev grabbed one of the men around the waist and slammed him into the ground.

"They why did you ask?" I lobbed another rock. This time, I was able to knock one of the men off balance enough for Sakev to take him down.

"Kill the alien scum!" Bastien ordered.

"*Kill.*"

"*Kill.*"

"*Kill.*"

"This is beginning to annoy me," Sakev threw another punch. Aside from knocking the men off balance, his punches didn't appear to be causing any pain or injury.

"We have to get out of here!"

"I changed my mind," he grunted. "This is kind of fun."

"Sakev!" I shrieked.

"I know! I'm teasing!" Sakev broke away from the fray and grabbed my arm. He took off as fast as he could, practically dragging me behind him.

The animalistic shrieks of the group echoed behind us. I looked over my shoulder. They were close behind.

"If we go straight to the clinic, they'll just follow us," I yelled. "We have to lose them first."

"Say no more!" Sakev took a sharp right down an alley.

I nearly lost my footing.

"Fucking hell, Sakev," I grumbled. "There's a person attached to the arm you're dragging."

"Do you want to lose them or not?"

He turned down a few more streets and alleys before doubling back to the road we were originally on.

There was no sign of Bastien and his followers, but we still ran like hell back to the clinic.

"Guard the entrance," Sakev ordered the officials as we stumbled into the building. "If you see men with dead eyes and lead pipes, shoot them down."

"You don't have the authority to give orders," an official huffed.

"If you aren't going to protect the people in the clinic, then why are you here?" I demanded.

"I wouldn't give her a hard time on this one, fella,"

Sakev backed me up. "You never know when you'll need her assistance."

"Fine." The official gathered a few others to take position by the door.

"Thanks," I panted. "I don't know what I would've done if you hadn't come along."

"Those humans have the audacity of rabid skrell. Attacking you just because they think I'm an alien?"

"Sakev, you *are* an alien." I whispered, laughter hurting my lungs. That run had done a number on me. I thought I was in better shape than that.

"But they don't know that," Sakev argued.

"I don't know how, but I think they do." I pressed a hand over a stitch in my side.

"That's impossible. The only time I take the holo-disguise off is in our room."

"Unless they have cameras in here." I meant it as a joke, but it made sense. I hoped that wasn't true. I was going to do a thorough search once I got back.

"Then they should be thanking us for the show we gave them the other night."

I blushed, but even memories of that night weren't enough to distract me from the situation at hand.

There was nothing normal about the way Bastien and his followers had acted. The assholes who attacked the clinic my first day here hated aliens, but they still acted human.

Shitty, but humans nonetheless.

There was more to it than just hating aliens. I was sure of it.

"Sakev, I have a morally ambiguous favor to ask you," I said. When he grinned at me, I felt a weight lift off my chest. Even though I was still upset about what happened, I felt bad for yelling at him back at the quarantine area. I still wished he'd talked to me, or even warned me, before firing his blaster.

But I understood that he felt it was the only thing to do. I was only thinking about my patients.

He was thinking about everyone's safety. mine included.

"That's my favorite kind."

Somehow, I didn't doubt that.

"You and I both agree that there's something seriously wrong with those people, right?"

"You mean, other than their blatant hatred of my kind?" Sakev asked.

"Yes. I need to figure out what it is." I wrung my hands and looked at the ground. "I need you to bring one of them here so I can examine him."

"Right. They already think I'm an alien. I'm sure they'll be more than happy to volunteer for a checkup," he snorted.

"I didn't say they had to come willingly."

SAKEV

I could hear the dressing down from Rhour and Vrehx already.

"No, I refuse. The people here already hate me, now you want me to stalk one of them and kidnap them?"

"Not one of the 'normal' ones, obviously," she argued back. "I need to know what's going on."

"I can tell you what's going on…I'm going to get arrested again." I lowered my voice so only she could hear. "Do you know how bad it would be for me, and you, if I captured one of them, and brought them back here for testing? Imagine, an alien kidnapping a human to be tested on. That doesn't sound cliché at all."

She tilted her head to the side and crossed her arms. "Wow. Didn't know you were a chickenshit."

"A what?" I asked.

"A *chickenshit*. A coward."

My eyebrows arched, and my jaw dropped slightly. "I am *not* a coward."

"Well, then, what's the problem?" She kept that mutinous look on her face, the one that said she wouldn't budge.

I threw my hands in the air. "Really? I just explained it. I can't just kidnap a human."

She unfolded her arms and poked me in the chest with her finger. "According to your own definition, they're not exactly human anymore. You shot those four back in quarantine without flinching. How come you're being such a wuss now?"

I opened my mouth, then shut it. I stared her down as she stared back up at me, her finger still pressed into my chest. My stare didn't work. She was insistent.

I gave in. "Fine. I'll help. But, just to let you know, those four in quarantine were already gone. These people aren't, so you're still asking me to stalk and kidnap someone. If I get in trouble for this, you cannot be upset with me."

"Whatever. There is something seriously wrong with those people, and not just mentally, so don't say it."

I clamped my mouth shut.

I was just going to say that.

She continued. "Something is affecting them, changing them. If we can figure out what's wrong, maybe figure out a way to help, then it'll all be worth it. I know you can do it. Please don't back out on me."

I put my hands on her shoulders and looked her straight in the eye. "This would be easier if you were taller," I teased. "Your idea makes sense, and if we can help people, then fine. I'll do it."

"Thank you. By the way," she said with a mischievous look on her face. "I'm just the right height. It's not my fault your people don't know how to stop growing."

"You like it," I returned, matching her tone.

"Meh," she said as she stuck out her tongue. I lowered my head and kissed her tongue. When she opened her mouth in surprise, I leaned in and snuck another kiss.

Well, snuck was the wrong word. The kiss lasted at least a minute. Then I broke it off, spun her around, and smacked her on the backside. "Get back to the clinic where Tona and the boys can keep an eye on you. I'll be back soon." As I walked away, a smile was plastered on my face as I ignored her jibes.

Her theory that the Xathi were behind the group's behavior wasn't a bad one. It was better than my idea that this was a town full of terrible human beings with deficiencies that had been dropped on their heads...often, every day.

I snuck out of the clinic and did my best to stay in

the shadows of the buildings. If I was found without my "escort" away from the clinic, I'd be thrown back into my favorite cell, or exiled from the town. While being away from this place wouldn't bother me in the slightest, Evie wouldn't want to leave without a good explanation as to what was happening here.

It took nearly an hour of sneaking around, not easy for someone of my size, before I found the group. They didn't seem to be acting normal, at least not normal for them.

They looked lost, out of sorts. Of the dozen or so that I found, they were walking around aimlessly in the yard of a half-ruined house. I noticed that when two of them bumped into one another, they snarled at each other, then tilted their heads to the side like they were trying to figure something out. It was as if they were trying to remember something but couldn't.

I started to worry, after an hour or so of watching, that none of them were in a position for me to get alone. I began to wonder how I was going to take someone for Evie to examine, when my luck changed.

One of them, a slender young man, barely out of his teenage years if I judged human ages right, wandered off behind the house. I snuck my way down the street a bit, cut across, and came back. In the minute it took me to get around to the back of the house, the kid had barely managed his way around the corner.

He saw me but made no noise. He just looked at me, opened his mouth as if to say something, then pointed his fist at me, as if he was trying to point, but couldn't open his hand. I allowed a moment to feel sympathy for him.

He walked towards me, making weird droning noises whenever he opened his mouth. When he was only a few feet away, he stopped. The look in his eyes changed. The droning noise stopped, replaced by a growl.

As he inhaled, I jumped at him, levelling him with a solid left hook that bounced him off the house.

He was unconscious before he hit the ground. I picked him up and carried him away. I was maybe a block away from the house, when I realized that there would be no way for me to sneak back to the clinic while carrying him. What was I going to do?

How could I get him to Evie?

Then, an idea came to me.

And Evie couldn't argue with me.

I ducked into an alley and laid the man down. I double-checked to make sure no one was watching, then I beat on him a little bit.

Just a bit. Not nearly enough for being a part of scaring Evie.

Then I picked him back up, walked out into the street, and started yelling for help.

"Someone, please help! He's been attacked!" I screamed at the top of my lungs in the most dramatic fashion I could muster as I headed towards the clinic. "Oh, help me, please!"

It wasn't long before I had a crowd of people asking me what had happened.

"He's been attacked! Some...thing...came out of one of the alleys and attacked him. Just started beating on him, trying to eat him." I let my voice tremble a bit. "It was terrible!"

"What was it?" a citizen asked.

"What attacked him?" someone else chimed in.

"Did you save him?" asked someone in the crowd.

"Where are you taking him?" shot a person to my right.

"Did you attack him?" an old man to my left asked.

That last question earned an "are you stupid?" look, and the old man who asked backed away.

I continued my act of drama. I began to get into the character as I had seen actors do on Skotan. "I don't know what attacked him. It looked human, but it had sharp teeth, and acted like an animal. I scared it away, but I don't know where it is." I let my voice become a little higher pitched, with a little more tremble. "It might not be the only one."

A few women screamed at the idea, while some men tried to comfort them with bravado. It brought a small smile to my face that I hid behind another round of yelling and screaming.

"Please, clear the way! I need to get him to the clinic. He needs medical attention. Oh, please, please clear the way!" The people let me through, some of them even clearing the way as an unofficial escort. We made our way through the town, with more and more people trying to get a look, asking questions.

I embellished a bit but kept my story the same. He had been attacked by some creature, some human with sharp teeth that had tried to eat him. I kept my voice loud, sometimes shouting out an answer to a question, but made it a point to keep yelling out that we needed to get to the clinic.

All the while trying not to laugh.

"Someone, please run ahead to the clinic. Tell Dr. Parr this boy's been hurt, been hurt real bad, and that she needs to be ready for him!"

A couple of boys ran ahead. As we got within a couple of blocks of the clinic, my guards arrived. They did not look happy to see me.

"Oh! Oh, thank the stars above. Tona! Skit!" I yelled. They looked at me curiously, never having seen me so overcome. "Please, oh please, help me get to the clinic! This poor boy has been beaten badly by some sort of creature, some sort of," and I made my voice serious for their benefit, "hybrid."

Tona's face fell as he heard the word, and Skit let out a curse. Skit started yelling at people to get out of the way, as Tona led me to the clinic. He cringed as I kept up my performance, but I had to.

My audience outside the clinic expected it.

And I was giving the performance of a lifetime.

EVIE

I wasn't sure what to expect when I heard two boys begging for my help. I assumed it had something to do with Sakev. I hurried with them to the lobby.

Nothing could've prepared me for what I saw.

Sakev, carrying an unconscious man slung over his shoulders like a sack of grain, stumbling through the clinic, flanked by officials.

"Doctor, please!" Sakev wailed. "This poor man! He's been attacked! I did everything I could! Bestow your mercy on him! He doesn't deserve this cruel fate!"

You've got to be joking. I didn't have to fake the shock on my face.

I knew I should've given Sakev more specific instructions. To his credit, whatever he was doing worked.

"What happened?" I asked Skit.

"He says a hybrid attacked the man." Skit looked ready to bolt.

"Bring him into the examination room at once!" I declared, my eyes wide as I clamored to make room for the victim.

"Doctor, can you save this man?" I half-expected Sakev to put the poor bastard at my feet as tribute. Instead, he laid the man on the table with exceptional care.

"Sakev's really taking this hard, isn't he?" Tona observed.

"If I'd been there just a moment sooner, this poor soul would've been spared," Sakev stared daggers at Tona, who looked cowed.

"Sakev, it isn't your fault!" I cried with the same affected dramatic flair, gripping his shoulders hard enough to turn my knuckles white. "Don't you dare blame yourself! I'm going to do whatever it takes to save this man's life."

"Sakev's a bit shaken, ma'am. I think a sedative might help him calm down, if you have some to spare." Skit looked so pale I was tempted to offer him the sedative instead.

"I'll get right on that. Will you see to the patients in the waiting area? Those poor people see something shocking every time they come here. It's a wonder they don't think this is a madhouse." Skit nodded and left, glad to put distance between himself and the unconscious victim.

"I can escort Sakev back to his room so he can recuperate." Tona offered.

"No!" I said quickly. "I, uh, need him here to deliver a witness account. He was the only one who saw the attack, correct?"

"That we know of," Tona nodded.

"Perhaps you and your colleagues could try to find more witnesses," I prompted. Anything to get him out of here. Tona hesitated. "Please! A man's life is at stake! The more information I can get, the better his chances are."

"Okay!" Tona hurried out of the room, muttering into a commlink.

I shut the door behind him and locked it before whirling on Sakev.

"What the hell was that?" I demanded. I wanted to look stern, but the ridiculousness of the situation got the best of me. I couldn't stop the laughter from bubbling up and spilling out.

I backed into the door, leaning against it for support as laughter wracked my body. I gasped for air like a fish out of water. Tears streamed down my cheeks. My stomach muscles began to ache.

"What's wrong with you?"

My inability to stop laughing made Sakev laugh, too.

"*What's wrong?*" I sputtered. "You're the one who has no concept of subtlety." I took deep, shuddering breaths to try and suppress my laughter.

Sakev opened his mouth to speak, but I raised a hand to silence him until I had more control over myself.

"Are you quite done?" His expression was somewhere between annoyed and amused.

"I might need an encore of that spectacular performance," I giggled. "I can't believe that worked."

"When will you start giving me credit? You, human females, are so difficult to please," Sakev teased.

A groan from the examination able shattered the humorous mood. The man on the table shifted, trying to lift his head.

"Where am I?" e asked. Sakev walked over to the table, considering the individual before him. "You! You attacked me!"

Quick as a flash, Sakev threw a swift punch, rendering the man unconscious once more.

"You know, there's a better way to do that." I pressed my fingers into the bridge of my nose.

"You want results? I give results," Sakev shrugged.

"I'd appreciate it if you don't permanently damage the subject's brain." I rolled my eyes.

"He's part of Bastien's gang. He's already brain-damaged." Sakev examined the bruised skin on his knuckles. "Why are you concerned for his well-being all of a sudden?"

"I'm not. It's just more difficult to get accurate results when the subject's brain is mush," I offered Sakev a gentle smile.

"Fair point." Sakev still wouldn't look away from the man on the table.

"Sakev?" I stepped closer and place a hand on his shoulder. "Are you okay?"

"Yeah. This human barely put up a fight." Sakev dismissed the man with a scoff.

"No, I meant with all the anti-alien bullshit that's flying around the city," I pressed. "People have been saying some really awful things, even though they have no idea what they're talking about."

"It's not a surprise," Sakev shrugged. "If the situation was reversed, I'd be just as aggressive toward outsiders."

"Maybe," I frowned. "But that doesn't mean it's right. Anyone who knows what happened in Duvest should understand that you and the *Vengeance* crew are here to help. If they're ignoring that, then I can only assume they're being willfully ignorant, and that will come back to bite them in the ass. Like it did with this fine gentleman here." I jabbed the man on the table in the ribs. A tad unprofessional, maybe, but I was sick of humans treating Sakev and his people as the enemy.

"That's the way it is sometimes." Sakev flashed me an unbothered grin. "If worse comes to worst, and someone tries to attack me, I can handle myself."

"They're already taking swings at you."

"Evie, all is well." Sakev's stern voice caught me off-guard. He softened, placing a hand over the one I was resting on his shoulder. "Your concern is appreciated, but this isn't something you need to worry about right now. Focus on the fool on the table."

I got the message. He didn't want to talk about it anymore. That was fair. I could respect that. Without thinking about it, I lifted myself onto the tips of my toes and kissed his cheek. Sakev twitched slightly, as surprised as I was by my actions.

I blushed, turning my attention to the man on the table.

Sakev came up beside me and gave my hand a quick squeeze.

"We've got to make sure he doesn't wake up again." I looked through the supply shelves in the room for anything that could help.

"I'm willing to punch him as many times as I need to."

"That's exactly why I want to stop him from waking up in the first place." I'd found a few syringes loaded with a sedative. "This is how you knock someone out. Actually, I believe you're familiar with this tactic." I injected the man with a low dose sedative.

"Let's get his shirt off." I tugged at the thick, rough fabric of the man's shirt.

"Wait, what?" Sakev took an alarmed step back.

"All of Bastien's followers covered their skin. I bet they're covered in crystal patches," I explained. With Sakev's help, I lifted the shirt off our unfortunate subject.

Sure enough, his skin was covered with big splotches of crystal coating. "I knew it!" I couldn't help but feel a small flourish of satisfaction bloom in my chest. We'd found another piece of this complicated puzzle.

"So, the anti-alien humans are Xathi hybrids?" Sakev peered closer, his gaze filled with disgust.

"It appears so. But it's speculation at best," I sighed. " It's not like we can keep kidnapping people for more data."

"That sounds remarkably like what I said before you sent me out to kidnap this man." Sakev quipped.

"It was a necessary kidnaping!" I said defensively.

"And you call me morally ambiguous," Sakev tutted.

"I think it's safe to say I'm just as morally ambiguous as you." I started pushing the man, trying to roll him onto his belly.

"The first step to overcoming a problem is

admitting it." Sakev stepped in, and quickly flipped the man for me.

"As much as I love our back-and-forth, we've got a bigger problem than my personal gray areas." I spotted a visible lump at the base of his skull and reached for a mask and gloves, scowling until Sakev complied.

It felt just like the lumps I'd found on Marigold and the others, except this man didn't have the thick layer of protective crystal growth.

"Agreed. Xathi hybrids. Got it." Sakev furrowed his brow. "So, the Xathi are likely influencing the anti-alien groups."

"Yes, but I think there's more to it than that. The four patients in quarantine progressed to an advanced state of hybridism overnight. Bastien and his followers have been operating for weeks and can still pass as mostly normal people. It's as if they were infected, and the infection hit a specific point before it stopped progressing."

I was missing something, I knew I was. I could only hope examining the bodies of the quarantined patients would be illuminating.

"Maybe there're multiple forms of hybridism," Sakev suggested. "I've no doubt that the Xathi had something to do with what happened to the four in quarantine, but they were different from the hybrids that attacked me and my team. We haven't got a good look at the hoards surrounding the city, either."

"And we still don't know how it spreads." My head had started to ache. "We can't hope to contain it, let alone reverse it, until we know that."

"There's one thing we know that has to take top priority." Sakev's tone was bleak.

"What's that?"

"Hybrids are already inside the city."

SAKEV

When we made it back to our room, Evie immediately set about checking every nook and cranny.

"Evie, what are you doing?" I asked.

"Checking for cameras."

"I was teasing when I said that." It was cute watching her scurry under the bed, ensuring her search was as thorough as possible.

"I know." Her head popped out from the other side. "But if hybrids are in the city, who's to say the people who put us in this room aren't afflicted?"

"What a deeply unsettling thought. Thank you, Evie." I flopped down on the bed, making it shake on top of her. She scrambled and crawled beside me.

"It's no more unsettling than everything else we've discovered since coming here," she commented.

"You. That *you've* discovered," I corrected, patting her hand.

"Thanks." She stretched out on the bed beside me. "But I haven't discovered nearly enough. I feel like every time I figure something out, it sprouts ten new problems."

"As a doctor, this can't be the first time you've run into a mystery." I rolled so that I could look at her. She mirrored my actions. "What do you normally do in a situation like this?"

"I've never been in a situation like this." She lifted her eyebrow.

"You know what I mean." I absentmindedly tucked a strand of hair behind her ear.

"Usually, I'd collaborate with my colleagues, look up past cases with similar symptoms, and research medical databases. I don't have access to any of those things here." Her voice grew soft and sad as she lowered her gaze. Everything that had happened since we arrived was starting to wear on her.

"You have me!" I made a show of looking offended. It seemed to cheer her up a bit. A soft smile appeared at the corners of her mouth. "I'm a colleague, aren't I?"

"With no formal medical training," she smirked.

"Does it make a difference?" I sat up and folded my

legs. "Come on, Madam Doctor. I'll start. This situation is more out of hand than I anticipated. The anti-alien group and the hybrids are definitely linked. The ones in the quarantine area were hybrids, too, but they were different, as are the ones I encountered in the forest. What does that mean?"

"Different strains." Evie sat up, too. She scooted until she was directly across me, then tucked her legs underneath her.

"Hybrids in the anti-alien group makes sense. There's a common enemy there who just happens to be the crew of the *Vengeance*," I sighed. "It's a solid infiltration tactic, but I don't understand why the Xathi are doing it."

"What do you mean?" Evie tilted her head. Her long hair was unbound for once. It spilled over her shoulder when she moved. I reached forward and ran my fingers through it.

"Xathi are physically superior to humans in every way. They don't need fancy infiltration plans to wipe out this planet. So, why are they bothering?"

"It was only the one ship that fell through the rift, right?" Evie pressed. "A piece of the hive mind is separated from the rest. We've had a few victories against them. I guess they aren't used to that."

"The total Xathi population is huge, but if additional Xathi can't come through, then it would make sense that the ones trapped here have turned to a less risky form of warfare." It was a solid theory, but it still didn't fully fit. "By now, the Xathi have learned that Skotans, K'ver, and Valorni are capable of beating them in a fight, but not humans. It still doesn't explain why they haven't stripped every city yet."

"That does sound strange," Evie mused. At this point, I knew what needed to be done, but I knew Evie wasn't going to like it.

"I think we should leave in the morning." Her head snapped up, eyes blazing. She opened her mouth to argue, but I cut her off. "General Rouhr needs to know what's happening, and if hybrids are in the city, I don't trust that our comms aren't intercepted. The sooner we tell him, the sooner we can organize an evacuation."

She paused. I don't think she expected me to have a well-thought-out plan. To be fair, I rarely did.

"Right now, there's no way to make sure a hybrid doesn't end up on the *Vengeance*. I can't leave when I'm so close to a breakthrough. I still have to examine the bodies of the quarantine patients. I'm so close to figuring this out, Sakev. I know it," she pleaded. "If you feel like returning to General Rouhr is the best course of action, then you can go. But I need to stay here until I know I've done all I can."

"You must be serious about this if you're willing to

let me make the decision," I teased. Her tense expression faltered, and a small smile broke through.

"You're thinking things through for once. I figured I'd give you the benefit of the doubt," she said.

"Finally." I let out a dramatic sigh. She rolled her eyes. "I think I'm going to stick around, if it's all the same to you." Her eyes brightened.

"Oh, really? How'd you come to that decision?" She looked up at me through her eyelashes.

"Something about you makes people keen to attack you, and I can't have that," I traced my fingers along the soft skin of her arm.

"Why not?" She tilted her head again. I don't know if she knew how adorable that little gesture was.

"I'd sleep much better at night knowing you're safe and sound," I replied in earnest.

"I'd rather you stay here, too," she admitted. "It's harder for you to get into trouble under my supervision."

She leaned forward, closing the gap between us and pressing her lips to mine. I wrapped my arms around her, pulling her into my lap. She giggled against my mouth. I slid my hand under the back of her shirt and placed it between her shoulder blades. She snaked her small hands around my shoulders, one grabbing a gentle fistful of my hair.

"Wait!" She suddenly pulled away. I looked at her,

confused and a little dazed. It was so easy to lose myself in kissing her.

"Are you well?" I managed to make my brain work long enough to form words.

"Yes, just one thing." She fumbled at my utility belt.

"In a hurry, are you?" I laughed.

She quickly found the device that generated the holo-disguise and switched it off. "Are you sure you don't want to take human Sakev to bed?"

She tossed her head back, laughing before taking my face—my real face—in her hands.

"I like *you*, you goof." She kissed me again.

"What's a goof?" I asked. "Is it another word for dashing, handsome, and brave?" I preened.

"In your case, I'm going to say yes. Now be quiet." She shifted so her legs rested beside my hips. I slipped an arm around the small of her back, closing the gap between us. I kissed her fervently, relishing the honey-sweet taste of her mouth.

With one swift motion, I lifted her shirt over her head and lowered her down on the bed. I paused between kisses to remove my own shirt.

I took my time wanting to learn every plane and curve of her body. Her breasts filled my hands. I let my fingers stroke over the soft flesh surrounding her nipples and then licked the rosy disks. They went taut, sticking up at me. I bent my head and subsumed one in my mouth, sucking it between my teeth. I bit, softly, at that crest.

Her fingers yanked at my hair. Her whimper made my body go hotter still. I gave attention to the other nipple, letting my fingers squeeze her breast as I suckled it.

Her belly sucked inward when my hands traced down it. I stared, fascinated, at her navel. I dipped my tongue into the indented flesh and she struggled against me. I asked, "I'm sorry, did that hurt?"

"No, it tickles."

I travelled further downward. The smell of her body, sweet and a little salty, came to my nose. I stroked a finger over her outer lips and they parted to reveal a deeper pink set behind them. The auburn curls at the junction of her spread thighs, glistened, tempting me to taste.

Evie gasped and bucked upward. My hands grabbed at her thighs, pushed her back down.

Her hips arched again and I moved one hand so that I could use it. I kept licking at her clit as I pushed first one finger into her body, withdrew it and then pushed two fingers into her flesh.

Her walls loosened, gave me entry. Her taste, her responsiveness set me on fire. Her hardened clit throbbed against my tongue, her inner folds milked my fingers. Pleasuring her gave me pleasure, more pleasure than I could have ever imagined feeling.

"Now," she moaned as her hips pressed her body closer to my mouth. "Now."

I knew exactly what she meant. I came back up along the length of her magnificent body and entered her in one swift motion that made her chest lift and drop in a long inhale and exhale.

Glorious.

She was glorious, and perfect, and mine.

She could scold me all she wanted, but I knew she trusted me. It was written all over her face as she looked up, her auburn hair fanning out on the pillow like the rays of a dark sun.

She dug her nails into my back, urging me on with her hips. I obliged, never taking my eyes off her.

Her eyelids fluttered and closed as she took her bottom lip between her teeth. She was nearing her climax, I could feel it building through her body.

Gently, I pulled her bottom lip from between her teeth.

"Look at me," I said softly. Her eyes snapped open and locked into my gaze.

A shuddering moan tore from her lush lips, and as she spasmed beneath me I lost control, driving into her, desperate to be closer, then the world went white with my own release.

Panting, I held her against me as she trembled.

I rolled off to the side before I collapsed on top of her.

Evie curled into my side, wrapping her slender arms around my torso.

As she drifted off to sleep in my arms, I realized how far I'd go to keep her safe.

EVIE

I walked into the clinic long before we were ready to
open and headed straight for the quarantine room.
Dr. Larkin was scheduled to return today. He could
take care of the morning's patients while I tried to solve
this puzzle.

Even dead, the bodies had changed. There were
even more scales on their skin. I went to Marigold's
body first, remembering how scared and nervous she
was when she first came in. She had complained of
headaches, and eventually admitted to me that she had
been hearing a woman's voice.

She looked so peaceful lying there. Just shy of
nineteen years old, she had had her whole life ahead
of her.

I brushed her hair off her face, then moved my hand

to the back of her head. The node was larger now, more pronounced.

A quick cut at the base of the skull showed the node fused to the bone.

Shit. I tried to scrape some off with the scalpel, but the blade broke. I used a pair of tweezers, pliers, and even grabbed a small hammer to try to knock it off the skull, or to at least crack it a little bit.

Nothing worked.

I gave up trying to break a piece of it off and moved on to trying to examine the thing. I grabbed a portable imaging scanner and brought it over to the crystal. The screen on the scanner went berserk. The colors changed so often that it made my eyes hurt. I took the scanner away and everything was fine, except there was nothing in it.

It was as if the scanner had been erased.

I put the scanner away, grabbed another, and experienced the same problem. I rolled her over to one of the more advanced imaging machines and it nearly exploded. It had gone completely haywire. Something wasn't right about any of this. I checked the other three, found the same nodes on them, and had the same issues with the scanners. I was so frustrated, my head hurt.

I decided to go about it the old-fashioned way and do a personal examination. The crystal on the back of Marigold's head was faceted, roughly a half-inch in size, and had a faint glow that seemed to emanate from within. The more I looked at the crystal, the more I thought I saw something…little veins coming out and burrowing into the skull. I grabbed a magnifying lamp, put it over the node, and looked more closely.

My head hurt badly, but I ignored it. The crystal seemed to be growing, almost as if it was alive.

A voice called me. I looked up, but no one was in the room except me, and the four bodies. I shook my head. I was imagining things. I examined the other crystals and found the same thing. Each crystal seemed to be growing.

I pulled away, blinking my eyes to clear them. I couldn't see straight. It had been four hours since I had started, and the clinic was now open.

I looked around the room and tried to focus on one of the warning posters plastered on the wall. My vision cleared, and I tried to go back to work.

"Doctor?"

My head snapped up, and I looked around the room. No one was there. I clicked the comm to the front desk.

"Yes, ma'am?" a voice asked.

"Yes. Did you or anyone else try to get ahold of me?" I asked.

"No, ma'am," she answered. I hung up and went back to work.

In the four hours since I had started, Marigold had

developed six new patches on her skin. I measured each one and documented what I found.

"Doctor?" There it was again. I looked around, but there was no one there.

"Hello?" I stood up, looking everywhere. "Is anyone there?" There was no one there. Just me. Me and the four bodies.

Four bodies that were sitting up.

Marigold had pushed herself up and was looking at me.

"Doctor?" It was the same voice. Her voice. "Doctor?"

I knew she wasn't alive, none of them were, but there I stood, with all of them sitting up and looking at me. They all had their heads turned to look at me. "Doctor?" they all said at the same time.

"Doctor Evie?" I spun around as fast as I could to see Marigold standing. "Doctor Evie? Why did I die? Why did you let me get killed? I thought you said I was okay. Wasn't I okay?"

"Doctor Parr?" I turned to my left, it was the old man. "Doctor Parr, why did you let me get killed? I came in to see you for a headache, and you let me get killed. You told me the headache was no big deal. You told me I would be fine."

"Doctor? You said I would be okay. I had a lot of

work I needed to get done," said the city official, who sat on the exam table that I had laid him on.

"No, no, no. This isn't happening. You're all dead."

"Of course, we're all dead. That's why we're asking you why we were killed. Can you tell us why?"

Oh God, the dead girl still had a teenage attitude.

"You're! All! Dead!" I yelled at them. The room was spinning. My head hurt, my stomach felt queasy, and I couldn't focus. "Why are you here? Why can't you just stay dead?"

I tried to walk away from them, but they just kept on talking. "Why did you let that red man kill me?"

Red man? What did they mean by *red man?* Were they talking about Sakev? How did they know that he wasn't human?

"What do you mean, 'red man'?" I asked. I grabbed my head, it hurt so much. I couldn't figure out what was happening.

I squeezed my eyes shut to block out their voices. I could still hear them. They kept asking me about why I let them be killed, why the red man killed them. My head throbbed. My eyes hurt. I was dizzy.

I couldn't think straight anymore. There was nothing left in my head, but their voices. I couldn't think of anything other than it, their dead bodies walking around. I dropped to my knees and tried to block them out.

I tried to think of other things, tried to force happy memories back into my head, but every memory I had had these four bodies in the background. Every memory of my family was perverted with them turning into hybrids and Marigold questioning me. I couldn't even remember...*what* couldn't I remember?

I couldn't even remember what I was trying to remember. I stood up and forced my eyes open.

The bodies were back on the tables, dead like they were supposed to be. There was no one in the room, no voices, nothing.

Everything was gone.

There were four tables with four bodies, but nothing else. Not a room, a floor, walls, ceiling, or anything. It was all gone. Just replaced by gray, gray everywhere. The bodies on the tables were completely covered in scales, in gem-like scales. Their faces were gone, replaced by a Xathi mask.

I couldn't catch my breath. Everything I was seeing was wrong. I knew it was wrong.

I tried to force reality back into my mind again. I thought about the lab, forcing myself to recreate the lab in my head. The door had been on the east wall, the computers on the west. The exam tables had been arranged in the center, with Marigold closer to the computers than the other three. On the north wall, there had been cabinets filled with beakers, chemicals, meds, and instruments that I had managed to get when we set up the new clinic after the attack.

My mind cleared, just a touch.

The attack. Maybe that was the key.

I thought about the people who had come into the clinic and harassed my patients. The damage they had tried to cause, about the fear they had created, about the carnage they had wanted to perpetrate.

I remembered how Sakev had stepped in, how he had stopped them, how he had saved everyone from the monsters.

I remembered how he had put himself between me and them.

I remembered how he had walked into this lab and shot the four people inside. I remembered how he had said it was necessary, how he had to because there was nothing else we could do for them.

Sakev that brought me back. It was the memory of him, how he was there for me, how he was there for his team, how he was always turning on humor to hide something.

The lab snapped back into view, with the bodies where they were supposed to be.

I was being corrupted, infected.

I had to be.

It was the only explanation.

I looked over at the desks where the computers

were, saw a notepad with a pen nearby. I had to leave a message for someone.

Who?

Sakev. I had to leave Sakev a message. To get me away from here, to get me as far away from everyone as possible because I was sick. He had to get me away.

So...I wrote...him...a...

SAKEV

I watched Evie leave the room.

I knew she thought I was still asleep, but I had learned long ago that to sleep deeply could result in death. One of my many nights sleeping on the streets when I was little had taught me that.

It was early when she left, much earlier than usual, but I knew she wanted to get some work done in the quarantine lab.

I had my own work to do.

Tona and Skit wanted me to show them how the neuro-grenades work and how to make them.

First, we'd need to learn if this city even had the necessary manufacturing capabilities, but we'd work something out.

I always figured something out, even if it was a little sketchy.

Why Nathan hasn't been around lately? I wondered as I drifted back to half-sleep.

Or at least I tried to.

I didn't exactly sleep, more like dozed off.

My subconscious decided to distress me again.

I was surrounded by the people that I had killed here in town: the rabble-rouser who had attacked the clinic and then the four people in quarantine. They accused me of killing them for no reason, and my dream-self argued back. I knew I was dreaming, but I couldn't stop it.

The five of them went away and were replaced by people that I knew from home, people that I had killed with my own hands, people that I had had killed, and people killed when the Xathi had attacked.

I forced myself back awake, in a crappy mood.

One sure cure for that.

Seeing Evie.

I grabbed my pack and headed for the clinic.

People let me be, but a few waved at me and greeted me as I walked by. It was refreshing to know that some people were okay with me, even if they still didn't know what I really was yet.

I made it to the guard station before the others, but I

was lucky—the night crew had been notified about me and knew I was coming.

I spoke with them and found out that the anti-alien group had been active last night, roaming the streets.

One of the guards, the one in the tower, had sworn he had seen a Xathi out on the edge of the forest, but his partner couldn't corroborate—he hadn't seen anything.

It worried me a bit, made me wonder what was happening.

Evie and I were certain that the hybrids were already in the city and that Bastien's group was controlled by the Xathi.

We just couldn't figure out how or why.

Were the Xathi trying to take over the cities from the inside, save their ammunition from the frontal attacks?

Was the whole thing a distraction from something else?

However, I didn't get much more time to think about it, as Tona and Skit showed up along with the guards of the day crew. They were only slightly surprised to see me there already.

"Looks like you were up and about early," Tona said as he logged in. Skit followed. "So, anything interesting last night?"

The question was directed at the night crew, but I answered instead, repeating what they had told me.

The night crew nodded and only added a few other things in regard to random drunks and one of the spider creatures.

I still hadn't learned what the skrell those things were called.

With a nod, Tona looked at the night crew. "Want to earn a little overtime?"

They all nodded. "Good. Sakev? You ready?"

"Yes, sir," I responded with a nod. I pulled out one of the neuro-grenades and laid it on the table. I had disabled it last night so it wouldn't be dangerous.

"This is a neuro-grenade," I started. "It is specifically tuned to the Xathi nervous system. We have several different styles of grenades that can paralyze, disorient, blind, and disrupt their neural connections to one another. We've had enough battles to have a whole bunch of trial and error on things that work."

"Neural...what?" one of the night crew asked.

"Neural connections. The Xathi are a hive-mind species. They are connected to a queen and communicate instantaneously with one another—sort of like how your arm and brain are connected," I explained. "Think about how your own body parts move. You rarely have to think about a movement before making it—it just happens. Your lungs breathe without conscious thought, your eyes blink, your heart pumps blood. They just happen."

I saw a lot of nods around the room.

"Xathi communications are the same way, or at least that's what we speculate," I continued. "These grenades interfere with those connections."

I spent the next hour explaining how the grenades worked and how to utilize them. I even gave Tona and Skit the schematics so they could work on making their own.

That's when I decided to ask about Nathan.

Skit dropped his gaze and stared at something on the floor. Tona shuffled from foot to foot, obviously trying to come up with an answer, or excuse.

"You can tell me," I cajoled. "Think of all that we've been through together. Think of all the good times we've had and all the stories we've told one another."

"But we haven't done any of those things," Skit responded. Then he got the joke and gave me a sort of half-grin "Oh."

"Yeah...we really should spend time together. There are so many stories I could tell you," I started.

Tona interrupted me. His voice was a bit sad and professional. "Nathan is no longer a member of the Guardsmen. He resigned shortly after the clinic attack."

That caught me by surprise. I pressed for more information, but Tona and Skit wouldn't budge. I decided to let it go and went about showing them how they could assemble one of the grenades and how they could modify it for a wider, shorter-lived blast, or a longer-lasting, more concentrated point of impact.

It was getting close to lunch when I realized that I hadn't heard from Evie since she left.

I made sure I was okay to go to the clinic and, with Tona's permission, I headed that way. I noticed one or two people following me as I made my way over, but I ignored them. If they were hybrids, which I was betting on, they were everywhere anyway, and one or two following me wouldn't be that unusual, at least not anymore.

I got to the clinic and walked in. I said hello to a few people inside and headed to the reception desk. The young girl at the desk, whose name escaped me, smiled at me. "Hi, Sakev. Here to see Dr. Parr?"

"Yes."

"She's in the quarantine lab. Want me to call her and let her know you're coming?" She was exceptionally peppy and very friendly, and cute, too.

I flashed her a smile, and she blushed.

"Let me surprise her," I insisted. "It's more fun that way."

She giggled as she buzzed me through the double doors that led to the elevators, and I headed that way. I took the elevator up to the lab and rushed to unlock the quarantine room.

Evie lay on the floor.

I rushed over to her. I immediately checked her pulse and was relieved to find out that she was still alive. She was only unconscious.

I tried to wake her up in every way I knew how. I lightly, and then not so lightly, slapped her cheeks. I yelled at her.

I got a small glass of water and splashed her with it, but to no avail. I was on the verge of a panic attack. I kneeled down and picked her up. She was cold and still, a piece of paper clutched in her hand.

"Xathi...mind control...crystals...hybrids...losing her mind...dead talking?"

What in...? I tried to make sense of her note.

Then I remembered my own dream and everything we had talked about.

She must have been scared she was being controlled. The note indicated to get her away from everyone.

I'd seen the other doctor when I came in, and there were volunteers here that maybe could help...

But Evie had asked me to get her away, get her out.

If she was right about being infected, controlled somehow, that was the thing to do.

And even if she wasn't, she'd asked.

She trusted me to help her.

Cradling her to me, I thought fast.

I couldn't take her out the front, but there was a side door I'd noticed that no one seemed to use.

I took her down the nearby stairwell and headed for it. I pushed us through the door and hesitated for a second or two as I adjusted to the sun shining in my eyes.

As soon as my eyes were clear, I realized that I had made a mistake. Bastien and his followers were there, waiting, snarling, growling at me.

With Evie in my arms, I couldn't fight them. Not and keep her safe.

The door was closed behind me, the alley to my left was filled with hybrids, and Bastien was in front of me.

"You…you…you not human," Bastien said. His voice startled me. It echoed within itself.

"Fuck off," I snarled at him.

Huh. I had been around the humans for quite some time if I was familiar with their lexicon of swear words.

He reached for me. I kicked at him, and then at a few of the others as I tried to push my way through.

Bastien's hands grabbed me, his nails scratching down my arms and to my belt. He grabbed a hold of my belt and pulled, intent on dragging me into his circle of friends.

There was a small popping noise, and my holo-disguise shut down. Bastien let go of me and I took that opportunity to run.

I ran as fast as I could with Evie in my arms, dodging in and out of alleys.

I had to figure some place to go, and then I remembered that we had flown over some old buildings on our way here. One of those places might work.

I ran. I knew I was exposed. I knew people would see me, but I had no choice.

"Hybrid!" I screamed, and I could begin to hear panic in all quarters.

As I got to the edge of town, Tona and Skit were there, staring at my giant, red-skinned body running right at them. The other guards raised their weapons, but Tona and Skit ordered them down.

I nodded a *thank you* to them.

"Hybrids are all over the city," I warned them.

"We've been getting reports," Tona said.

"From everywhere!" Skit added.

"Take this down," I instructed Skit, then recited coordinates near the *Vengeance*. "I'm from the forests in that area. They're patrolled. Try and get as many of the townspeople to evacuate as you can."

Both nodded.

"Thank you," Tona said sincerely, "for everything."

"Hybrids!" a guard down the line yelled.

"Go!" Tona yelled to me. "We'll handle things here and keep them from you."

I nodded to Tona. He had started as the person to guard me.

Now he had seen me in alien form and had thanked me.

Perhaps there was hope for the humans in this town, after all.

Tona nodded back, then ordered the guards to prepare. I could hear weapons cocking as I ran out the gate.

I could only think of running as far as I could, as hybrids tried to follow us. The trees were a blur, the animals more so, but all I had in my mind was getting Evie to safety.

It was nightfall when we made it to a small collection of buildings.

I went for the sturdiest looking one, a small cabin, and forced my way in. I laid Evie down on a bed and went back to the door to close and block it.

I could hear things moving in the forest.

It was going to be a long night.

EVIE

Wake up, little one.
There's much work to be done.
You need to wake up, my lost little lamb.
Wake up.

I knew it was bright before I opened my eyes. I braced myself, opening my eyes slowly to a bright winter sun.

My fingers lazily traced up and down one of the planks of the smooth, sanded wooden bench I sat on.

I looked down at my bare feet, my toes barely touching the wooden deck below me. I shifted my weight, the bench rocking forward and back again at a lazy drift.

I knew this place.

I looked out to the never-ending field of waist-high

grass, shimmering like an ocean as it rippled with the wind.

This was my home.

I grew up here with my mother, father, and sisters. My parents were botanists. They moved to this large piece of land so they could have enough space for their specimens. My sisters and I would spend whole afternoons playing hide and seek in the tall grass.

"Awake at last," the melodic voice I'd heard before I woke up sighed in my ear.

Alarmed, I turned to find the most striking woman I'd ever seen. Though she was sitting, I could tell she was tall.

Maybe even as tall as...

I grasped for a memory, but found nothing.

My father was tall.

Yes, that must've been what I meant.

The woman's arms were long and thin, and her skin was the color of bleached bone. Her narrow shoulders were concealed behind a cloak of snow-white hair that reached the deck floor. She looked at me with bright eyes that held no true color, like stars or diamonds.

What surprised me the most was the gown she wore —pure white and spotless. It looked as if it were made of layer upon layer of delicately spun insect wings.

I'd never seen a gown before, only pictures from the

past that had survived the journey from Earth. The curious child in me wanted to stroke it.

I didn't think the woman would be angry with me, for she seemed so kind.

"You can touch it," she encouraged. I blinked in surprise. Could she read my thoughts?

I reached out and traced a finger along the edge of her skirt. It felt like silk and mist. Her pale lips pulled back into a smile, revealing a row of pointed teeth.

I took my hand away from her skirt.

"What am I doing here?" I asked, looking out to the grassy field.

I didn't want to look at the woman.

I didn't want to see those teeth again.

"This is your home, isn't it?" she said. "Don't you like it here? Haven't you missed it?"

I did miss it. I was sad when my parents sold the house and the surrounding land to move to Glymna. That was long after my sisters and I left the nest, though.

"Yes, this is my home."

Where had I been all this time? Surely I wasn't always here.

I remembered my parents leaving. I left, too. I know I did.

But where did I go?

I must've done something. It had to have been

something very important, or else I wouldn't have left this beautiful place.

What was it?

Movement in the grass caught my eye. Something was moving through the towering blades. Every once in a while, the wind would blow just right and reveal what looked to be the top of a dark head.

"Evie, you're it!" a high voice called from the grass.

"What was that?" I asked, looking at the pale woman.

"I believe your sisters are waiting for you." The woman was careful not to bare her teeth again, but I could still see them when she spoke. "Don't you want to play with them?"

"My sisters are taller than the grass." My voice sounded light and airy. "My sisters are both grown and married."

The pale woman's brow furrowed.

"Are you certain, little lamb?"

Little lamb… I turned the phrase over in my mind, grasping for the memory it belonged to.

Yes, that was it. My mother used to call me that.

My mother also had names for my sisters. Gwyn was the little firefly, and Nedla was the little sparrow—creatures from Earth. My parents appreciated our root planet.

"Why wouldn't I be sure?" I asked the pale woman.

"They're my sisters." Her tight-lipped smile was tense and cold.

"Of course," she conceded.

The dark heads in the tall grass vanished.

My sisters stopped asking me to play. That was unusual. Something about this wasn't normal, but my thoughts were sluggish and slow to take form.

I watched the grass sway in the breeze. I didn't want to talk to the pale woman anymore. I wanted to get back to what I was doing before, but I couldn't remember it.

If I let my vision fall out of focus, the grass looked like an enormous pool of golden honey. The color reminded me of something...of someone.

"This place always looks so much lovelier in the springtime, doesn't it?" the pale woman prompted.

Suddenly, bright green sprouts wove their way up the porch railing. Fat, fluffy yellow flowers burst into bloom.

I knew those flowers. My parents tried to grow them, but they didn't take to the environment. They were called marigolds.

Something twitched in my mind. A memory struggled to form, but I couldn't see it. The honey color of the grass grew deeper and richer as the pale sunlight gave way to the brightness of a spring afternoon.

"You're going to drive yourself mad if you keep

thinking of the past," the pale woman soothed. She placed an icy hand on my shoulder. Her skin didn't feel right—it felt like a smooth, polished stone—and her grip was firmer than I had expected.

"Relax. Sleep under the warm sun. Smell the flowers," she urged, but there was an edge in her voice now.

"I was doing something important," I murmured.

"Like what, little lamb?"

My head was in the pale woman's lap. I didn't recall lying down. She stroked my hair with slender fingers cold enough to send shivers down my spine.

Something deep inside me urged me to run...

No, not run...but to go back.

Back to where?

"There's nothing here that will harm you, little lamb. You should sleep." The woman began to hum, but the song was all wrong. It didn't soothe me—it frightened me.

I craned my neck to look at the honey-colored grass once more. Something about it pulled at my mind.

That color meant safety. It meant trust.

I started at the swaying grass, unblinking. A shape took place in my mind.

It was an eye, the same rich color of the grass. With the eye came a smile, then a laugh.

Sakev!

I remembered him. We were together last night. Wasn't it last night?

How long have I been here? I didn't see him in the morning. I went to do something.

What was it?

"Perhaps you prefer summer to spring, hmm?" the pale woman spoke again, and I felt something sharp skitter through my mind. It hurt.

The pale woman's eyes were filled with fury, though she kept her serene smile in place.

Sakev...

Where was he? I needed to tell him something.

I left him a message someplace. It was important. I hope he found it.

Around me, the grass fields paled and dried up. The blue sky turned dark and bleak as thunderheads blocked out the sun. The marigold blooms shriveled and fell at my feet, brown and crunchy.

Another memory came into me: a small-boned girl with eyes like a doe—Marigold. She was young and sick. She came to see me.

She was dead now.

There were others...three others...four total...four dead.

An icy claw pierced my mind. I flinched, putting distance between myself and the pale woman.

She didn't look lovely anymore. Her teeth grew longer. Her eyes were larger and more sunken.

There was another painful jab in my mind, like it was searching for something. If it penetrated deep enough, maybe it would find what it was looking for.

I remembered Sakev, Marigold, and the rest. There was something in my memories this pale woman wanted. But why?

She stood suddenly. I could see now how unnaturally tall she was, how too thin her limbs were. Her glowing white hair now looked stringy and thin.

I couldn't believe I'd seen her as beautiful.

"Sleep!" she shrieked.

The deck and bench below me cracked. The porch gave out completely. I scrambled backward, now able to see her for what she was.

I knew at that moment, with absolute certainty, that I was looking into the eyes of the Xathi Queen.

"You won't take my mind!" I screamed back. "I know what you are!"

The Queen's howl was deafening.

I squeezed my eyes shut and put all of my energy into keeping my mind away from her claws. I focused on building a wall, brick by brick, higher and higher until I could no longer feel her jabs.

Any moment now, I expected to feel her hands on

my throat, but they never came. Her shrieks grew more distant as I forced her out.

I had to get back to Sakev.

I remembered now.

I had left him instructions to get me away from the clinic. I hoped he would heed my instructions, for once.

Somehow, I would get back to him.

SAKEV

If I'm not the most worthless person around, I have to be on the short list, I thought as I watched Evie.

She thrashed around every so often, sometimes so hard she almost fell off the bed.

I looked around again. It was a small cabin. There was the main room that we were in now, a small storage closet at the back of the cabin, and a small bathroom across from it.

The kitchen wasn't much of a kitchen, just a small stove and a cold unit tucked into the corner. The only entrance to the cabin was the door we had entered and the two small windows next to it. Whoever had lived in this cabin had lived alone.

I wondered how long ago that was, as the layer of dust on everything was thick.

The bed that I had put Evie on was of good size and looked comfortable. I just hoped it was. With Evie's thrashing, I could only hope she wouldn't hurt herself on it.

With nothing else to do, I took off my holo-belt to see if I could fix it. I dropped it on the table and instantly regretted it as the dust flew into the air and into my lungs. I coughed for what seemed like forever before I cleared out my lungs enough to breathe.

I looked at Evie, worried that the dust might get into her lungs, as well.

Fine, I'll clean up the place, I thought to myself.

That was a funny phrase, *thought to myself*. Who else was I going to think to?

I chuckled a bit as I thought about that. Then my cheerfulness went away as I realized that that was how the Xathi held the advantage. They didn't have to hear someone give orders and then process the information before making a decision about it.

It was just like I had described to Tona and Skit and the guards—it was instant. The only Xathi I knew that needed to think were the queens.

"What have we gotten ourselves into, Evie?" I knew she couldn't answer, but I hoped that my voice might wake her up.

My stomach grumbled. I laughed at the sound.

I did a cursory search for food and found nothing

edible, unless I was suddenly able to eat wood. Just an empty canteen, long dried up and as dusty as everything else.

We had no supplies other than what I had in my pack. My comm unit and extra weapons were back in our room.

Skrell.

I came back to Evie and sat down on the bed next to her.

"You know, I don't think I had anything to eat this morning. Did you? I mean, I know you left early for work, but I hope you were smarter than me and actually got yourself something to eat."

I looked down at her. Her face was covered in sweat, and she seemed to be in pain.

"Hey!" I yelled as I grabbed her. Her skin felt cold, nearly ice cold.

"Evie!" I yelled again. There was no response.

"Skrell. What do I do?"

The only blanket in the entire cabin was on a chair by the door, and it was nearly disintegrated when I bumped into it when we first came inside. I had to get her warm. I crawled into bed with her and wrapped my arms around her.

She was so cold it made me shiver. "Strength, Evie. You will make it. No matter what is going on with you, you can beat it. I know you can."

I held her closer, hoping that my excessive body heat would warm her up. It was the only thing I could do, other than burn the cabin down, which would defeat the purpose of using it as a hiding place.

If this was going to be a hiding place, a bright glowing light sort of defeated that purpose. I untangled myself from Evie and turned off the glow-globe that had been illuminating the cabin. Then I crawled back into bed with her and held her close.

"Evie, Evie, I know you can hear me…at least I hope you can hear me." I wasn't sure what had come over me, but I just started talking.

"You told me about your family. But I didn't want to tell you about mine."

I hoped that the sound of my voice penetrated her mind, helped her somehow.

"I'm not the good guy. Skrell, I'm barely even lovable, if you really knew about me. As a matter of honesty, growing up, my home was not something I enjoyed or had fond memories of. My father, I don't remember much of him. He disappeared when I was very young. I never knew—"

I paused. I thought I heard something outside.

I kept quiet for a while, listening to see if the sound would get closer. But it didn't.

As soon as I was sure that it was safe to speak, I went on, "You know, when I think about it, I still don't know what happened to my father. My only real memory of him was when I was maybe four winters old. He had come home full of smiles, arms full of gifts. He had kissed my mother while we were opening our presents. They were happy, smiling. We all were."

I took a deep breath and remembered that day. It had been a very mild winter, one of the warmest on record. The winter industries were struggling because of it, but my father had somehow managed to find the money to get us presents and to keep our home when so many others were losing theirs.

He came home, singing at the top of his lungs, and handed each of us gifts, my mother included. I remembered hearing her gasp when she received a beautiful necklace. They kissed, they hugged, and they smiled.

Then father took us outside to play, and we played past our bedtime. We were happy that day.

Evie began to shake and thrash around again. I had to hold her tight and close to keep her from hurting herself. "Shh, it's okay. It's going to be okay. I'm right here. I'm right here, Evie."

I kissed the back of her head and held her close. I breathed in her hair, choked on it a bit, and carefully spat it out of my mouth.

Leave it to me to make a mess of something as simple as

holding a person, I thought as I kept telling her it was going to be okay.

"When my father disappeared, my mother changed. To keep food on the table and a roof over our heads, she worked two jobs. Her first job was in a market near our home, selling...I don't remember what she sold. It was her real job that ruined our childhood."

I took a deep breath. No one knew this. But I couldn't keep secrets from Evie. Not anymore.

"She forced us to steal. I screwed up a job once, and she kicked me out of the house. Can you imagine a child, a little eight-winter child, trying to survive on the streets? I almost died twice. The first time was that first week on my own. I had been attacked by a shopkeeper's pets, and if I hadn't been found by a passing soldier, I never would have made it to the hospital.

"The second time was after I got out of the hospital, that first night. I nearly froze to death. If I hadn't been found by the local crime boss, I wouldn't have made it through the night. He brought me in and cared for me. As payment, I worked for him." I proceeded to tell her the whole story of my life in crime, all leading up to the Xathi invasion.

Slowly, ever so slowly, Evie calmed. She stopped thrashing around and even stopped trembling. Her breathing was still shallow, but it was improved.

"Evie, I need you to stick with me. You're the only

one that gets me, sees me. I have to be funny, or my mind goes back to my past and I go back to hating everything about myself. I have so much guilt over everything I've done, over everyone I've hurt. I need to be funny to feel better about everything.

"Evie, you're the only one that makes me feel normal, the only one that makes me feel as though I'm not worthless. I..." I stammered. I couldn't believe what I was about to say, the feelings that revelation was bringing to fruition. "I..."

"Sa...kev?"

She was awake.

EVIE

Sakev had done what I asked: he brought me to an abandoned shack somewhere in the middle of the jungle. I didn't know where we were. I wasn't sure Sakev knew where we were, either, but at least we were away from other people.

I wasn't sure how long we'd been here. After I woke up, I remember seeing Sakev's face smiling over me.

I remember he kissed me, sweet and gentle.

I didn't get a good look at our location before I passed out again. Since I broke away from the Xathi Queen, I'd been exhausted.

I didn't dream about the tall grass or my childhood home. I didn't see the Xathi Queen again. I don't think I dreamt at all.

The next time I woke, I was able to see that we were

in a cabin. Sakev and I talked, but I don't remember what was said. Sleep took me over quickly, and the cycle went on.

At one point, I told Sakev to record how long I stayed awake and how long I slept.

I jolted awake once more.

"How long was I out this time?" I asked. Sakev was by my side in an instant, helping me sit up and bringing a tin cup of water to my lips.

"Less than an hour." He grinned. "That's your shortest sleep yet." I fumbled for the datapad to add that time to the list, then shuffled off to the small enclosed wash room.

By the time I collapsed back in the bed, my legs had gone wobbly again.

The first time I woke up, I said Sakev's name and then immediately passed out and slept for another ten hours. Less than one hour was progress.

"Sorry I keep leaving you alone." I lifted my arms overhead to stretch the stiff muscles. "You must be getting bored looking after me."

"Not really." Sakev positioned himself so that I was propped upright on his chest. "I can finally get a word in when you're passed out. We've had long, productive conversations while you were unconscious."

A witty remark was poised on my tongue when something else tugged at my memory.

"I remember hearing your voice." I felt as surprised as he looked. "That's how I knew I needed to wake up." Sakev's face blushed as much as his vibrant skin color would allow.

"What did you hear?" he asked.

"You told me about your mother…and your father," I said thoughtfully. The details were coming back slowly.

"So, you did hear all that," he marveled.

"Thank you for telling me." I turned my head, wincing at the stiffness of my neck until my forehead rested against his cheek. "You deserved better than that."

"Thank you." He wound his arms around me, holding me tight. I didn't mind that it hurt a little bit. "So now you know one of my secrets. How about you tell me one of yours?"

"Like what?" I asked. I didn't have many secrets, certainly not like the one Sakev had been keeping.

"What happened while you were asleep?" he asked curiously. "You were thrashing about like a mad thing. More than once I had to catch you before you flung yourself off the bed."

"Ah," I uttered. I wasn't sure how I was going to explain what had happened to Sakev. I didn't fully understand it myself. "I was home again, sitting on the porch of the house I grew up in. The Xathi Queen was with me."

"Evie!" Sakev gasped.

"I think she was pulling information from my least protected memories," I continued. "She made herself look beautiful at first, like something out of a fairytale. I fell for it for a while. But then I remembered you, Marigold, and the others. She became enraged. She started stabbing at my mind, at my memories. It's difficult to explain."

"She attacked you physically in a metaphysical way," Sakev said suddenly. My eyebrows shot up in surprise.

"Yes, I guess that's the best way to describe it. How did you know?"

"Skotan females possess empathetic abilities, just like Jeneva. When they walk through your mind, you can feel them, even though they physically aren't touching you," Sakev explained.

I'd never spoken to Jeneva personally, but I knew her sister. Amira was rough around the edges, but I knew she had a good heart.

"That's incredible." I was struck by a pang of guilt for not asking Sakev more about his people. "Almost as incredible as the memory of you shattering her hold on me."

"How did you fight her off?" Sakev asked further.

"I focused on building a wall around my memories.

She couldn't break through it, but I felt her trying. I think I must've made the wall so big that I pushed her out."

I wished I could run tests on myself. I needed to see what kind of damage the Queen did to my brain.

"And she's gone now?"

"I can't feel her like I did before. But I only imagined shutting her out of my mind. What if she's still in there, hiding? How would I know?"

My thoughts were crashing into each other. I reached around to touch my neck. My skin felt smooth, normal.

But if the Queen was in my brain, could she stop me from noticing crystal patches or a crystal node forming?

"Evie—"

"Feel my neck!" I moved my head forward, exposing the base of my neck. "If there's a hard bump, you need to leave now!" I felt Sakev's warm fingers rest against my skin.

"There's no bump, Evie. You're fine." He tried to pull me upright again, but I wiggled away from him. The world spun on its axis, and stars flashed in my eyes.

"We need a plan." I was talking quickly. Had I always been able to talk this fast? "Symptoms can come on quickly...sometimes. We need to check every hour, make a log. Did I do anything a hybrid would do?" I was breathing too fast, but I couldn't get it under control.

"No, Evie. You just acted like you were having an extremely realistic nightmare. Which you were." He reached out and took my arm.

"But—"

"Evie." Sakev pulled me back into his embrace. "Evie, slow down for a moment. You've been through a lot. You should take some time to rest."

"I was locked in sleep by a xenophobic alien monarch. I don't need rest," I snapped.

"Fair point," Sakev conceded. "But I wouldn't call that sleep restful."

He was right. My bones felt like they'd been replaced with concrete, and my head ached. I signified my surrender by slumping against him.

"That's a good doctor." He patted the top of my head.

"Sakev, I may be exhausted, but I just fought off a Xathi Queen. So don't think for a second that I won't fight you, too," I grumbled. I felt Sakev's laughter rumble through his chest.

"I just had to make sure I was talking to the real Evie and not a clone."

"A clone would've killed you by now," I replied.

"Really? Because if I had to wager between the real

Evie and an Evie clone on who would kill me faster, I'd put money on you."

He planted a kiss on the side of my face, then another, and another, until he'd kissed every bit he could reach. I giggled and playfully tried to escape his kisses.

"So," Sakev spoke between kisses. "What was so memorable about me?" I twisted in his arms so I could look at him face to face.

"Do you really want to know?" Sakev shifted us so that we were lying flat on the bed, facing each other. "It was your eyes."

"My eyes?" Sakev looked perplexed.

"Were you expecting something else?" I asked incredulously.

"I never considered my eyes to be my best feature." Sakev shrugged. "It's not the most common color for a Skotan."

"For humans, unusual eye colors are often considered the most beautiful." I ran a hand along his cheek. "It's the same for you."

"Was that a compliment?"

"Don't act so surprised!" I laughed, stealing a kiss.

"Allow me to return the favor." He kissed me deeply, then gently pulled my shirt off and rolled me to my stomach. "You're tired. Let me do the work."

As he traced a line of kisses down my neck, my eyes drifted shut as I focused solely on his touch.

He ran his large, sturdy hands over my shoulders, down my arm, and back again, smoothing and soothing me, turning me to his touch. Every ridge and callous of his fingers set my nerves to spark as he grazed my bare skin. I wasn't sure if it was my exhausted state or my increased arousal that made me feel a little drunk.

Tiny kisses and nips, working down my spine like shocks, then soothed back again with his hypnotizing touch.

When he eased my legs apart, knelt between them, I sucked air into my lungs, the shattering sensations robbing me of speech. His fingers skimmed my folds, teased the tender flesh of my inner thighs.

His hands, rough and yet tender, traced upward again. My body quivered, and my toes curled as a whimper escaped my lips.

I didn't have to see his honey colored eyes to know he was smirking. "Is there a problem?"

My toes curled. I whimpered out, "Void, no."

"Good." Gently he coaxed me to my knees, his hands lifting my hips up, stroking my back until I rested head down, weight on my elbows.

With a sharp tug, he pulled down my undergarments. Another shuffle told me he'd yanked down his own as well. I wanted to look behind me, to take in the sight of him, but I kept my eyes closed and let the anticipation drive me wild.

I shuddered against him, his own arousal pressing against my backside. That hardness sent my senses reeling, made my thoughts fragment. Everything fell away except explosive desire. I squirmed against him until that hardness nudged against my bottom again, quadrupled that longing.

His hands grasped my hips then slid over my cheeks again. He separated them, and cool air met my wet and aching flesh. I bit at my lips and grunted out, "Don't tease..."

His cock rubbed against my core as I pressed backward but he kept himself apart from me. The air ran over my body again, adding a new layer of sensation and making my fingers curl into fists.

I gasped when he entered me, leaning over to cover my back with his chest, enveloping me in his world. I brought one hand up to touch the side of his face, to wind into his hair. His breathing was rough in my ear as he thrust deeper while putting his fingers to work between my legs. My senses kicked into overdrive until he was the only thing I was aware of.

My body jerked and my hand tangled more fully into his hair. His fingers grasped my shoulders, brought me backward and closer to him as he thrust into me again.

My whole body was in tune with his movements. I met every thrust and whimpered with each withdrawal of his body from mine. Every rub of his fingers against my skin, that hard and aching flesh at the top of my mound, made me gasp and moan.

This went beyond simple pleasure, this was something far better.

I gasped and rocked in his arms, pushing myself against him so I could take in as much as possible. I felt like it would never be enough. I needed more of him— all of him.

"Sakev," I shouted into the pillow. Stars exploded behind my eyelids as wave after wave of exquisite pleasure crashed over me. The world fell away, and I floated on a cloud, my limbs airy and weightless.

His body curled over mine. His fingers dug into my shoulders, pushed into the skin there hard enough to leave bruises. The pain was there but it was secondary to the aftershocks rolling through me and the feel of him stiffening, roaring above me. His strong thighs, the long flat muscles there, lay against the backs of mine and I felt his muscles jumping against my skin.

He dropped onto my body and drove it forward. I let out a little 'oof' and he muttered a quick apology. I lay there, stunned, mind still shattered.

He withdrew and then positioned himself next to

me. His hands stroked my shoulders, my back as he brushed my hair off my face.

Sakev pulled me in close, planting a kiss on the top of my head. "Are you all right?"

I gave him an amused glance. "Is that your way of asking if I enjoyed it?"

He gave me a quizzical look. "No, I meant are you all right. I didn't mean to hurt you when I fell down on top of you."

Laughter came from my mouth. "I'm fine. Are you?"

"Is that your way of asking if I enjoyed it."

The soreness between my legs and the stickiness there drew my attention. "If I had to guess, I'd say that you did."

He nuzzled his face against my hairline. "I did."

A yawn cracked my mouth open. I covered it with a hand. He cuddled me closer, holding me against his heated body.

I let a different sort of exhaustion pull me into sleep.

SAKEV

There was no food or water. Evie was weak from fighting against the Xathi Queen and needed food to regain her strength. *I* needed food.

Our...exercise...last night had drained what little bit of strength and energy we had, but it was worth it. She made me feel things physically that I didn't know I could feel. I only hoped that I had returned the favor... again, and again, and again.

I had been thinking about food. I forced my concentration back to figuring out our food-and-water situation. I had to do something.

The *Vengeance* wasn't far away. We could make it as long as we weren't attacked or chased by any Xathi or hybrids.

"Evie?" I hated waking her up, but we needed to figure out the day. "Evie."

She opened her eyes, rolled over a little bit, and smiled at me. She reached her hand up and placed it on my cheek. I leaned in, and we kissed.

"Morning," she said groggily. She was adorable just waking up.

"Good morning to you, too. We need to talk."

She leaned herself up on her elbow, a serious look on her face. "Oh? In the human world, that's never a good statement."

"What do you mean?"

"If someone says that 'we need to talk', it usually means bad news, especially in relationships," she explained. "You're not breaking up with me, are you?"

I smiled at her and let out a small chuckle. "If 'breaking up' means ending this relationship, no, I'm not. You humans are very unusual with your vernacular."

She nodded. "Yeah, I've never really understood common human language. It's very weird that we have six words that mean the same thing or six meanings for one word. It drives me nuts. But you were saying?"

"Yes. We have no food and no water. You're weak, and I haven't really slept or eaten in almost two days. And while we can survive a little longer without food, we need something to drink." I grabbed her hand and kissed it. "The *Vengeance* isn't too far away and—"

She interrupted me with a shake of her head. "No. There's a good chance I'm still infected, and I don't want anyone else to get infected, too."

"But you're not showing any symptoms of hybridism. I think you're fine," I argued.

"Really? And what exactly are the symptoms?" she asked as she put on her you-can't-possibly-be-this-stupid face. "We don't know what they are, so we can't be sure that I'm okay."

"I feel fine. I'm not having weird visions of little green men or dead people." Which was true, I wasn't. I just had bad dreams every now and then. "You haven't been experiencing anything since you woke up. Have you?"

"No. No," she said quietly. Her fight with the Queen still bothered her. "No more visions, no more anything. I don't remember my dreams from last night, but I know they were good dreams." She smiled at me. "Thank you for being there for me."

"Of course." I held her close to me, her head on my chest. After a few minutes, I spoke again. "But I need to get us something to eat and drink, at least."

She lifted her head and looked at me. "You could always go back to the *Vengeance* on your own."

"No. I won't leave you alone."

"But the crew needs to know about what we've learned and about what's happening in Einhiv," she insisted.

"And we'll tell them...together. I'm not leaving you behind."

"Sakev," she started, but I wouldn't let her finish.

"No. It's as simple as that," I asserted. "I'm not leaving you behind. Either we go back to the ship together, or we stay out here together. That's it."

She tried to say something, but I stared her down. I didn't care how angry or upset she got with me. I wasn't going to abandon her.

She gave in.

At least, I thought she had.

Evie laid her head back down on my chest, kissing it lightly. Her lips were so soft and gentle, and they felt good, too good.

But then, she didn't have the energy for this.

Only, as usual, she surprised me. Her mouth trailed downward just as I opened my mouth to utter a gentle protest. She found my organ and licked it softly. Her hand trailed down to the end of my shaft, right where it connected to my body. She ran her fingers lightly across the connecting skin.

I groaned. "You're tired."

She chuckled and said, "Not that tired, Sakev."

Her lips pulled me into her throat. I went stiff and hard. "I...you're going to..."

"I know," she said in a muffled voice and then she released me just to suck me back in again. Her tongue swirled over the base of my shaft. My body tensed and then went even tenser. The pleasure was intense, mind-shattering. I groaned as her fingers formed a fist around the lowest part of my organ and helped her to form a tunnel of heat and wetness around my member.

She stopped and then she straddled my body. I stared up at her, fascinated, as she worked her hips into position, her knees on either side of my body. She slid downward. Her folds cradled my flesh, clung to it as she lifted her hips and then slid back down. I caught a breath. My hands found her breasts. She leaned forward so her mouth could meet mine, our tongues clashing, dancing.

She worked hard and fast. This was not going to be a long and soft interlude. We strained together, our bodies desperate for release. A small dew of perspiration came up on her skin. I licked away the salty beads and buried my face in her breasts before letting my tongue and teeth play across her nipples.

Her hands went to my chest, flattened down against it. I stared at her face as a slow red flush climbed

upward from her throat and then into her jaw and
cheeks. Her hooded eyes and her parted lips made me
arch upward and grip her hips, pulling her down again
before lifting her up. The pace, not slow to begin with,
picked up speed. She rocked back and forth above me
then swung her hips in a deliberate little circle that left
me gasping.

I groaned out her name, and her folds took my cock
inside and milked the seed from me just as she came.
Her core clenched and loosened, fluttered and opened.

I couldn't breathe, didn't want to. My shaft pulsed
and her hips wriggled against mine and she made
another one of those circles. She raised herself, lowered
herself and took me in fully.

She body lowered until her upper half was lying
over my chest. Her hair spilled down her back, around
us. I tangled my fingers into the fine tresses, fisted it,
brought her face to mine for another soul-stirring kiss.

"That," she panted out, "Is what humans call a
quickie."

Had she said quickie, or quickly?

I decided not to ask. Luckily, I'd get a chance to ask
again.

Soon.

Instead, I gently grabbed her head, pulled her up to
me, and kissed her. Then I got out of bed and started to
get dressed.

"Let's make a compromise," I said as I pulled on my pants. "If you're not showing any symptoms of anything other than general human oddness tomorrow morning, we head back to the *Vengeance*. Yes?"

"Really? 'General human oddness', huh? You keep trying to be funny, don't you?"

With a slight side nod of my head, I shrugged. "It's a character trait. You know you love it. So, do we have an agreement?"

She sat up, letting the blanket fall slightly from her chest. It was an amazing view, even as she covered herself back up. "Deal. But," she said as she held up a finger, "if I show even one symptom, just one, I stay here."

"Okay. I think I can live here."

She looked shocked. "You would stay? Here? With me?"

"Unless you have a healthy clone I can stay with instead," I replied with a sly tone.

She reached behind her, grabbed a pillow, and threw it—all in one motion. I laughed as I caught it, with my face.

"You ass!" she yelled at me. Then she broke into laughter as I removed the pillow, a ridiculous look on my face. I laughed with her. It was good to see her in good spirits.

I reached into my pack and took out two blasters, as well as two energy packs each.

"What are those for?" she asked.

"You," I answered. "I'm going out for food and drink, and I'm not going to leave you here unprotected." She opened her mouth to say something, but I stopped her. "Don't argue with me. Not now." She nodded, and I showed her again how to load them. "I'll be back as soon as I can, okay?"

She nodded and slapped my butt as I turned around to get my swords and remaining blasters. I smiled at her and headed out the door. "Lock up behind me. I'll be quick."

I closed the door and waited to hear the bar drop into place. I trusted her to take care of herself and went searching the nearby countryside.

Over the next two hours, I found several plants that I had witnessed other animals eating, as well as some berries and other fruits. I actually had to fashion a small basket out of twigs and branches in order to carry it all.

I imagined what the rest of the team would say if they saw me with a basket full of fruits, berries, and plants, but I didn't care. As long as Evie was well, that's all that mattered.

I was reasonably certain that the stuff I had gathered wasn't poisonous or harmful. If what I remembered from Jeneva's lessons on the native plant life was right, we would survive with the food I gathered. All I needed to do was find water.

I trekked a little further away from the cabin and managed to find a small stream that four or five different animals were drinking from. Thinking that if they survived drinking the water, we would survive it, too, I waited until they were finished and gone, then went upstream and refilled my canteen.

The water smelled faintly of mint, a plant that I had learned was nearly universal around the cosmos. It grew around my house back on my home world, and from what I've learned from the humans, it grew on Old Earth, as well as here.

I headed back towards the cabin. I grew concerned when I saw the bodies of some forest creatures outside, but when the door opened and Evie stood there, a hand on her hip and the other on the door, I couldn't be any prouder. She had done well.

"You were a little busy, I see." I smiled as I walked up to the cabin.

She shrugged. "Well, someone had to keep the homestead safe while you were gallivanting and picking flowers," she teased.

"How was your trip, dear?" she asked as I walked inside. She closed the door behind us and dropped the bar back into place.

I picked up on her attempt at play and answered

back. "Just fine, dear. The sun was bright, the air was crisp, and things were good."

"Aw, I'm glad you were able to enjoy the sun while I slaved around the house all day," she joked. Actually, she hadn't been joking. The cabin was clean, cleaner than it was last night.

I kept the game going. "Gathering food is a time-honored tradition in many families. It's hard work making sure your family is fed."

She poorly held back a laugh. We both laughed as I laid out all of the plants, berries, and fruits that I'd found. Evie immediately began examining them, tossing some of my bounty into a waste receptacle near the stove.

I looked at her wide-eyed. She smiled back at me. "What? I don't want to die, and those are harmful to humans. Just saying."

I nodded. "That's fair."

"Oh," she said as she popped a berry in her mouth. She grimaced and pursed her lips a bit, one of her eyes spazzing closed as she tilted her head. "Ugh. Holy mother of...hot damn, that's sour! Whoa!" I laughed at her as she ran to the sink and turned it on.

"Skrell," I said as I pointed. "You fixed the sink."

She drank and swallowed, then turned the sink off. "Mm-hmm. That's what I was going to tell you before that berry tried to kill me. We have water."

"Well," I grabbed my canteen. "I suppose we don't need this."

We spent the rest of the day talking and playing a game Evie had dubbed *Will this kill me?* I don't think I've ever had so much fun just being...domesticated.

The world was descending into chaos around us, but for a few moments, we were happy.

EVIE

"I don't want to go," I whined, putting on a show of stomping my feet like a child and flashing my most convincing pout.

Sakev loved a good performance.

"We had a deal," Sakev repeated for the third time. "You aren't showing any symptoms of hybridism."

"But we still don't know what all of the symptoms are."

"Do you just want to stay here because you're proud of your innate homemaking skills?" He arched his brow.

"Partly," I admitted. "But Sakev, this is serious. The Xathi don't know where the *Vengeance* is. If I exposed the ship to hybridism—"

"I know." Sakev cupped my face in his hands. "But

did it occur to you that the *Vengeance* has the most sophisticated med bay on the entire planet? If we go back to the *Vengeance*, you can see definitive proof that you're not afflicted. Wouldn't that give you some peace of mind?"

"You're right." I couldn't argue that. After working in that run-down clinic, I'd been daydreaming about the med bay back on the *Vengeance*.

"What was that?" Sakev was bent over his holo-disguise, absorbed in trying to repair it.

"Oh, I said you're right," I repeated.

He looked up with a blank expression.

"I'm sorry, one more time?"

"You're—" I realized what he was doing. "I'm going to throw my shoe at you."

"It's such a rare thing to hear!" He put his hands up in defense. "Forgive me for wanting to savor it."

"I'm letting you off with a warning this time," I teased.

"I just thought of another reason why going back to the *Vengeance* is a good idea," Sakev said brightly.

"And that would be?"

I couldn't see his face anymore. There was a fifty-fifty chance this wasn't a legitimately good reason. Make that sixty-forty.

"Best quarantine pens on the planet!" he exclaimed.

I flung my shoe. It would've been a direct hit if he

hadn't unsheathed his protective layer of scales. It bounced off his broad back as if I'd thrown a balled-up piece of paper.

In a blink, he was on his feet, rushing toward me at full speed.

"Wait!" I squealed.

He locked his arms around my waist and lifted me off my feet, slinging me fully over his shoulder.

"Put me down!" I laughed as I thumped my fists against his back. His scales felt like a solid piece of armor.

"You throw a shoe at me and then dare to ask for mercy?" Sakev spun around in small circles.

"I'm going to be sick! Do you really want to walk through the jungle with my last meal all over your back?"

Sakev quickly placed me on my feet and held me steady while the room stopped spinning.

"You're pretty fun to throw around." Sakev brushed my hair back into place.

"You're pretty fun to climb on, you big oaf." I lifted myself onto my tiptoes to give him a quick kiss.

"Keep that up, and we won't be leaving here anytime soon." He winked.

I walked to the bed, letting my hips sway. I tossed my hair as I sprawled across the bed, the perfect picture of seduction. Sakev's eyes roved over my body.

"What are you thinking?" I tried a wink of my own, but I didn't have his charisma, though by the look on Sakev's face, it didn't matter.

"I'm thinking that you're trying very hard to get your way." Sakev murmured. "Unfortunately, it's not going to work. We've got to leave soon if we want to make it back by nightfall."

"Damn it."

I knew he was right about returning to the *Vengeance.* It was the smartest course of action, but I still hated the idea of boarding the ship without being completely certain I wasn't bringing hybridism on board.

"I'll carry you out if I have to," Sakev warned. "You know I'm capable."

"Could you do that anyway?" I asked, still sprawled on the bed.

Sakev looked back over at me and smiled. He crossed the room and scooped me up in his arms, then carried me out of the room, walked a few paces, and set me down on the forest floor.

"What the hell, Sakev?" I quickly got to my feet.

There were lots of large monsters in the forest looking to make a snack out of me, but there was also plenty of creepy crawlies down in the dirt that I wouldn't want to meet, either.

"I got you started!" Sakev beamed. He swung his

pack over his shoulder and started walking. "Let's move, Madam Doctor!"

And so we said goodbye to the little cabin that had been our haven.

"Don't worry." Sakev gave me a gentle nudge. "When this is all over, we can come back. It's a nice spot for a romantic getaway."

"I'd like that."

I laced my fingers through his as we walked. We moved cautiously at first, expecting something to jump out at us at any moment.

Between the hybrids, Xathi hunting parties, and the natural creatures of the forest, traveling on foot was a small step up from a suicide mission. But the forest was unusually quiet as we walked.

"This is easier than I expected," Sakev said after walking for over an hour with no conflict.

"I was thinking the same thing." I looked up to the canopy, half expecting a perfectly camouflaged jungle cat to leap down at us.

"If the hybrids have been stalking this area, maybe the animals migrated."

"It's possible. But something doesn't feel right."

A thick branch snapped in the brush a few feet from us.

"What the hell was that?" I grabbed for Sakev's arm, my heart pounding under my ribs.

He stood impossibly still, listening to the sounds of the forest. Another twig snapped off to the right. Sakev lifted his blaster in the direction of the sounds.

"Out of all of the things that live in this forest, what percentage of them want to kill us?" Sakev whispered.

"Like eighty-nine percent or so."

"So, the shoot-first-ask-later mentality is the most responsible option?"

"Do you have any weapons other than the blaster?" I asked.

"No. Most of my heavy-hitting gear was confiscated by the officials in Einhiv."

That's right. Well, I hoped the officials were getting some good use out of them. It wasn't a secret anymore that Sakev was an alien.

"Then yes, shoot first." I agreed.

He fired a few rounds into the brush, scaring a flock of birds from the trees above. Slowly, Sakev stepped over to where he'd fired. He pushed aside the leaves.

"There's nothing here."

He waded a few feet deeper into the forest, just to make sure, before turning back to me. He looked at me, then stopped suddenly, dropping his blaster on the ground.

"Sakev, what is it?" I asked.

"Stay perfectly still, Evie." Fear gripped my throat. "You're going to be okay, I just need you not to move."

Fear gripped my throat.

He crouched down slowly, not taking his eyes off whatever was behind me.

Then I felt something tap between my shoulder blades. My spine went ramrod straight.

I knew Sakev had told me to stay still, but I couldn't help it.

I looked over my shoulder.

"What the hell?" I leaped toward Sakev, putting some distance between myself and...I wasn't sure what it was.

The creature before me stood on two legs, like Sakev and me.

From the body proportions, I guessed it was female. Her deep blue skin had an iridescent quality to it, silvery where the mottled light of the canopy touched her. Rather than hair, she had a bony frill that rose up from her forehead and followed the curve of her skull.

Her eyes looked like galaxies, deep and dark but generously speckled with flecks of light. Surprisingly, her nose was in similar size and shape as my own. Even more surprising, I didn't see anything on her face that resembled a mouth.

She stared at me, unblinking. In her hands was a silver spear, incredibly thin and topped with a hooked point. The entire length of it boasted minuscule and impossibly detailed carvings I couldn't make out from here.

"Evie, duck!" Sakev's voice startled me back to the present.

I instinctually jumped to the side. I wanted to tell him to wait, but it was too late.

He attacked her.

SAKEV

I jumped between Evie and the creature and knocked the weapon from its hands. I threw a punch, another punch, and another punch before finishing off with a round-house kick. All of them missed.

The thing...this blue-skinned, starry-eyed something or other, moved as though it floated on air. Its movements were so fluid, it was like fighting water.

I threw a backhand and a punch, but it evaded easily. And when I tried to be sneaky and kicked out at the what I thought was a knee, it moved its leg out of the way with the same speed and fluidity.

I felt my own intelligence drop. This thing made me look stupid.

I kept attacking. I heard some yelling, but I wasn't

paying attention. I was trying to keep this thing away from Evie, and I was so insanely frustrated that I couldn't land a single blow, not even a graze.

This creature dodged everything that I threw at it. I even hurled insults and, I swear, it evaded those as well. Nothing seemed to work on it.

I felt something touching my arm, and I looked down to see Evie's hand. I stopped. My breath was quick, but I forced myself to calm down.

"She's not a threat to us," Evie said.

"If it's not a threat, why didn't it say something?" I asked. I had completely missed something important, I could see it on Evie's face.

She sighed, shook her head, and looked me in the eye. "Because *she* doesn't have a mouth, genius."

I stared for a minute. She'd said "she."

"Uh, how do you know it's a she?"

Evie threw her hands in the air and slapped my arm. "She has breasts, stupid. Would it kill you to be a little more observant?"

Breasts? I looked back at the creature. I made sure to take my time to really look at it.

Evie slapped my arm again. "Pig."

I didn't know what a "pig" was, but I was positive she had just insulted me. I feigned innocence. "What?"

"You were staring. Be nice!" She turned back to the

creature and pantomimed an apology as she said the words "I'm sorry."

"Hey, why are you apologizing?"

"You were attacking her, you insensitive clod."

Again, I was sure she had insulted me. "She attacked us!"

"How?"

"She popped out of the bushes and pointed that, that..." I stammered a bit as I tried to figure out what exactly her weapon was. "Well, she pointed *that* at us."

"Aww, did the scawwy cweatuwe scare you? Poor baby."

She turned away from me and looked at...well, that.

I was hurt, but not by the creature, obviously.

It hadn't laid a single hand, or appendage, or whatever, on me. It had simply dodged everything I threw at it...her. My pride had been wounded more than anything.

I tried to apologize but closed my mouth at a dirty look from Evie. She had been trying to communicate with the creature.

"Is there something we can help you with?" she asked her.

The creature tilted her head to the side in what I guessed was amusement. That was when I noticed that she didn't have a mouth.

"Did you notice the lack of mouth? I don't think she can talk," I said.

"Wow, really? I hadn't noticed." The sarcasm that dripped in that statement was a slap to the ego. "I'm still gonna try."

"Understood." I backed off a step or two and observed.

Within several minutes, I had counted to at least six hundred in my head while Evie tried to talk to the creature. She had even tried some form of hand movements that I had never seen before, but it was useless. The creature didn't respond.

Evie gazed back at me, a look of resignation on her face. "I don't know what to do."

"Well, my attempt at dancing was a colossal failure." My attempt at humor brought a grin to Evie's face as she shook her head. "Maybe we try to write something down?"

Suddenly, the creature reached out with her hand and touched Evie's head. Evie's eyes fluttered shut and her head leaned back. I jumped forward and the creature took her hand off Evie's head.

"What the hell did you do?" she snapped at me.

I was taken aback. "I was trying to defend you. Was that wrong?"

"She was trying to communicate. That split-second

she touched me, I heard her speaking to me." Evie fixed me with a hard stare. "Don't interrupt."

I held up my hands in surrender and took a step back.

The voices of my past made fun of me for being intimidated by a female a head shorter and a whole lot lighter than me, but I reminded myself that human women were feisty, dangerous, and vindictive.

I had heard stories of how Jeneva and Leena had dealt with Vrehx and Axtin when they angered them. I didn't want to see how far Evie would go.

Evie motioned for the creature to try again. It was a sensational effort that held me back.

I didn't trust this creature, but I trusted Evie.

She put her hand on Evie's head again, and Evie's eyes fluttered shut once more. After a minute or so, the creature pulled her hand away. Evie shook her head to clear it, then looked at me.

"This is how she communicates with people not of her kind. You should try it." Evie took a step back.

I shook my head in earnest. "No. I don't want that thing in my head."

"What do you mean? How else will you talk with her?"

I pointed at Evie. "You. That's how."

"Seriously? Big bad Sakev is scared to let something connect with him?" There was a hint of sadness in her words, as if she thought that maybe she was included in that statement.

"Connecting is fine, but I don't want anything *in* my head, rooting around in my mind. No." I shook my head furiously. "No. Not a chance."

Evie shook her head. The creature watched us, her head tilting to the side every so often.

Evie let out a loud sigh. "Anyway. She's from the *Aurora.*"

My eyes went wide, and I looked between the two of them. The *Aurora?* That was the empty ship that had crashed a little bit ago on the island of Kangeti.

"The *Aurora?*" I repeated out loud.

"Yep, that's the one. It's her ship. Well, it's her people's ship, to be more precise."

"Her people?"

Evie nodded. "Yep. Apparently, she's not the only one."

"Where are the others? Why was it empty? Where are they from? How did they get through the rift?" I guess my excitement got the best of me. I couldn't stop asking questions.

"Easy there, tiger," Evie laughed.

Again, I wasn't sure what a "tiger" was, but I smiled an apology nonetheless.

Evie continued, "She hasn't told me all of that yet. We're just starting to build a rapport."

"Well, what are you waiting for? Talk to her."

"Oh, so it's okay for her to be in my brain, but not yours?" She winked at me.

I shot her a dirty look, and she laughed at me. She reached out for the creature's hand, and after grabbing it, placed it on her head. Her eyes fluttered shut again.

I was prepared to stand there and watch for however long we needed, but Evie's eyes opened while the hand stayed on her head.

"She says we should probably move somewhere else. A small herd of Luurizi is heading this way, and we're right in their path."

I had to search my memory for what a Luurizi was, but I followed the females as they walked off the pathway. Within a few minutes, the creature's premonition had proved correct.

The Luurizi, the small, delicate creatures with antlers and spikes on their hooves—I think one of the humans had likened them to something called a "deer"—bounded past us.

I looked at the creature in astonishment. Could it predict the future, or was it simply able to see things better with those unusual eyes? I thought about it as she and Evie "spoke" to each other.

I could see Evie's eyes shake and move under her eyelids, and sometimes her mouth moved as if she was speaking. It was unusual to watch a conversation happen without sound. The only sound I heard was the retreating Luurizi herd and the local birds chirping again.

After nearly an hour of their still, silent "conversation," the creature took her hand from Evie's head.

Evie's eyes met mine, flashing with urgency. "We need to get back to the *Vengeance.*"

SAKEV

Sakev

We got back to the *Vengeance* to find it in a state of mild chaos.

Perfectly normal.

Team Two had returned a few minutes before us and were in the middle of turning in their gear to the ship's quartermaster.

"We need to get you to the infirmary," I said to Evie as I helped her through the hangar bay.

A few nods and light waves from crew members greeted us as I took her through, but those same nods and waves became stares when they saw Fen.

I turned to one of the crew. "Let General Rouhr know that we've returned, and that we've brought a potential ally. And tell him that we'll be in the infirmary."

He nodded and ran off while I took Evie and Fen to the infirmary. We had a small group of followers by the time we got there, as everyone wanted to see Fen.

I helped Evie up onto an exam bed and let the ship's AI begin the examination. The AI was nearly done with the examination when the General walked in, my team with him.

"I'll be right back," I whispered to Evie and walked over. "Sir."

"Would you care to explain why you brought an unauthorized entity onto my ship and into my infirmary?" Rouhr was not happy.

"My apologies, sir. I should have had Team Two take Fen into custody, but I made the decision to bring Evie to the infirmary in order to get her taken care of."

Rouhr looked at me. "Based on the unknown name, I'm going to assume that belongs to your unknown guest. Again, would you care to explain?"

I nodded. "Yes, sir. According to Evie, Fen here—"

"According to Evie?"

"Yes, sir. Fen only speaks through your mind and I—"

"Vrehx, place her in a holding cell immediately and don't let her read your mind!" He looked at me. "What were you thinking, bringing a telepath onto my ship? Do you realize the security implications?"

I held up my hands to stop him. "She doesn't read minds, sir, not without physical contact."

His eyes went wide. "Don't let her touch you!"

"Sir, she's on our side. Her people were on board the *Aurora*. She only survived because she was still in stasis, that's why she wasn't affected by the Xathi attack that caused the ship to come down."

He absorbed what I had told him for a few moments, then looked at Evie and the medical AI.

"How long before she's able to move around again?" he asked the AI.

The system glitched a bit but answered the General. "The pa-pa-patient will be released from care in forty-eight minutes, Ge-ge-gen-general Rouhr, sir."

"Fine." He turned to look at me. "You have forty-eight minutes to get the both of you something to eat, then meet me and the team leaders in the conference room. I want both of your reports."

"Yes, sir." He left, and I turned to Evie. "How are you feeling?"

"I'm okay. Are you in trouble?"

I shrugged and smiled at her. "No more than usual. It'll be fine. Anything you're interested in eating?"

"Yep. Food."

I smiled. "Good answer. Be back in a few minutes."

I left and headed to the galley, grabbed us a small
tray of food to share, and headed back to the infirmary.
I thought about Fen being locked up just because she
was different, and while I wasn't happy with it, I
understood the general's sense of caution.

I walked back in and with a big flourish, said, "I'm
back! Did ya miss me?"

Evie smiled back at me. "What took you so long? I
damn near starved to death waiting for you."

The AI responded, "The patient is in-in-in-in-
incorrect. She is nowhere near starvation."

Evie and I laughed and enjoyed our snack before we
headed up to the conference room. Inside sat the General,
Vrehx, Sk'lar, Karzin, and every member of all three teams.

Rouhr directed us to the two empty seats, and we
sat. "Report."

I started. I told about how we got into town. Vrehx
shook his head at my impulsive decision to jump, and
what happened afterwards.

I left nothing out, except the personal stuff.

That was between Evie and me.

I detailed my conversations with the guards, my
run-ins with Bastien and the anti-alien group, and my
fight with what Evie and I had agreed were hybrids.

Rouhr held up a finger to stop me. He looked at
Evie, "Can you tell me about the hybrids?"

Now it was Evie's turn. She told everything, including her own fight with the Queen. This brought out numerous questions from everyone. Evie and I answered all the questions.

"Sir?" I asked.

"What is it, Sakev?"

"What are we going to do with Fen? She can be a reliable ally," Evie said before I could. I nodded and pointed at her with my thumb.

"We don't know her. We don't know her intentions, and we don't—"

Evie interrupted the General, something the rest of us wouldn't do. "With all due respect, General Rouhr, you don't know her, but I do. I've been talking to her and learning about her, her people, and her story. She can open and close the rift, sir. She wants to help us end the Xathi."

"Why?"

"Because it was her people that originally created them, and she wants to fix that mistake," I answered.

That started a big argument between everyone about whether or not Fen was trustworthy, if we should keep her locked up, or if we should kill her.

"Kill her?!" Evie yelled over the rest. "We can't kill her! Is this really how you would treat an ally that can help us against the Xathi? By killing her?"

"Dr. Parr, I don't think you understand the situation."

Rouhr's calming tone sent her ballistic.

"You want to kill her just because you don't know her. You're being a damn hypocrite!"

"Excuse me?" he shot back.

She stood up and walked toward him. "You bring us in, us humans, and you let us stay. You let us work. You let us help. But when someone who can *actually* provide some assistance and turn things around, you want to kill her. If you do that, you might as well kill me, too."

Her eyes narrowed. "If you can't trust her because she's a telepath, what about Jeneva? Honestly, if you're just going to suspect her because she's an unfamiliar alien, you're not much better than those panicked fools out in the city."

Her jaw tightened. "You can't have it both ways."

She was standing next to him, her short little frame against his gruff, old exterior. I nearly laughed at the sight but held myself in check. This was not the time for me to try to be humorous.

She glared at him. Their silent war had quieted everyone, and we just sat and watched.

Luckily, we didn't wait for long. Rouhr grinned and nodded.

"You're right. I have allowed the humans on the ship

with little to no scrutiny, and now I'm not extending the same to this new ally. Commander Vrehx?"

Rouhr looked away from Evie for just a moment.

"Please let our guest out of her cell and bring her here. It seems that there is much that needs to be discussed."

He looked back at Evie and laid a hand on her arm.

"My apologies, young lady. If I could trust you to look after my men, I should have trusted in your judgment as well. Please sit. We still have more to discuss."

"Thank you," she said lightly as she came back to her seat.

"Now," Rouhr said with a breath, "based on your... contest...against one of the Xathi queens, do you believe that this infection, or mutation, or perversion, whichever word best fits the situation, is reversible?"

Evie leaned forward. "I'm not sure. I haven't yet discovered how the...let's go with mutation...works. Everyone that I examined in Einhiv was already too far gone, and I was unable to examine the crystal at the base of their skulls before I faced my own issues."

With a heavy sigh, Rouhr sat there and digested the information. I looked at Evie and gently grabbed her hand, trying to reassure her.

"Sakev?"

"Yes, General?" I answered.

"Do you believe that there are people in Einhiv that have not yet been corrupted?"

"Yes, sir. I do. What did you have in mind?"

"Talk to the team leaders. Let them know the layout of Einhiv and the people whom you trust there. Also, make sure they know what to look for regarding the hybridism. If there are any people we can save, we need to save them."

"Thank you, sir," Evie and I said in unison.

Karzin spoke up. "Sir? I don't believe bringing more refugees here is a viable option. We're already taxing the system as it is."

Rouhr held up his hand to stop anyone else from speaking. "I understand. But we must be realistic. We are no longer fighting a war against the Xathi, we're losing it. We need all the allies we can get, and if there are any humans in Einhiv, or any other city, that are not yet infected, we need to find them and find a way to work with them."

"Work with them how, General?" Karzin asked.

"We only have two choices. We either find a way off this planet and through the rift, closing it behind us, or we stay, fight, and hope that we live long enough to find out their master plan. To do either, we are going to need help."

Evie spoke up, "And, as much as we're not fighters,

humans are pretty damn resourceful. We can definitely help."

A small discussion started up after that, mostly between me and the team leaders about Einhiv and its people.

I looked over at Evie, who was talking with Rouhr, and we smiled at one another. I wasn't sure if we had a plan or not, but we had a beginning.

Maybe.

SAKEV

The meeting in the conference room had not been what I had expected.

It left a sour taste in my mouth, even if Rouhr had agreed to listen and try to work with Fen.

I went back to the infirmary to prep everything for whoever the teams managed to bring back. They were going to Einhiv and try to convince as many people as they could to return to the *Vengeance* with them. I wasn't sure who or even how many the teams would be able to bring back, so I worked with the AI and prepped as much as I possibly could.

General Rouhr had assigned me several crew members to help. I had even managed to get the AI working again without its little stutter-glitch.

That evening, I went to where I usually slept and

found that all of my stuff was missing. I searched and searched but couldn't find it. I asked around, but no one knew where my things were.

I started panicking. I ran to find Sakev, and one of the crew told me that he had gone back to his room. I ran to his room, knocked on the door, and entered when it opened.

I found out where my stuff was.

"What the hell?"

He looked at me and shrugged. "What? You live here now." He went back to arranging his things to make room for mine.

"Wh-wha-what?" I stammered.

He looked up from his things. "Wow, you've really improved your vocabulary since we got back to the ship. Are you sure you're smart enough to be a doctor?"

"What did you just say?!" I nearly shrieked.

I was still a bit peeved at the idea that he had moved my stuff. I wasn't upset that we were going to share a room. I was just upset that he had assumed that we would and that he had permission to move my things.

"Easy there, Shrieka. These rooms aren't so big that you can shriek without hurting people."

I took a step back. "Wa-wait. Who's Shrieka?"

He sat down and looked at me. "Ancient Demoness of Destruction, if you believe the old tribes. Most of us just use her name when someone gets to be a bit too loud."

I just looked at him like he was in idiot, which he was. But he was *my* idiot.

I threw my hand onto my hip and tried to stare him down. "You do know that moving my things in here without my permission is a serious violation of my privacy."

"Please. I was inside you. How much more privacy invasion could there be?" he cracked at me.

"Hey! That's impolite!"

"What's your point?" He didn't even have the nerve to look ashamed for his actions and words.

I was angry, if only for a second. "You're an asshole."

"So you keep telling me. But you know you're happy to be here, or am I that far off in my assumptions?" He smiled and patted the bed.

I took his suggestion and sat down next to him. He looked over at me, his customary smile missing.

I put my hand on his leg and looked up into his eyes. "What's the matter?"

"I'm about to say your favorite line." He forced a small grin, but I knew he wasn't happy about it. "We need to talk."

"Okay. What about?"

"About what General Rouhr said in the meeting." He

moved further onto the bed before sitting cross-legged in the middle.

I mirrored his position, so we could look at one another.

"Okay."

"I'm not completely sure you and the others realize what he meant when he said that we are losing this war," he said dourly.

I gave him the customary look that he had earned from me whenever he said something stupid. "You really think that humans have never had war, or been on the losing side of a war? Granted, as far as I know, we're the first humans to make what we call 'alien-contact.' But there have been so many wars throughout our history, it's nearly a hobby for us."

"Plus," I added with a drop of sarcasm, "I do have eyes and a brain. I can figure things out, and it's not hard to realize we're probably losing. The Xathi outnumber your crew, and they're assimilating my species."

He shook his head and looked at me sadly. "No. It's not just that. Have you seen this ship fly?"

"Well, I saw it crash. Does that count?"

He chuckled. "Not exactly. Too many of the broken components are buried at the bottom of the ship, and we have nothing that can lift it up enough to get to them. See, the *Vengeance* wasn't meant for atmospheric flight."

"So...that would mean..." I couldn't finish my question.

He nodded, slowly. "Yes. The only way for us to get off this planet is to somehow fix the ship, and that would mean revealing where we are. That would put us under constant attack, and we would never have the time to fix it. The General knows this."

I sat there and tried to digest the idea. That meant that what we were doing was pointless.

Why did we spend so much effort on saving everyone? Why had we been trying so damn hard?

No. I couldn't let myself be dragged down that rabbit-hole, so I didn't.

We would figure something out. Humans had always managed to find a way to make things work. It was how we'd survived.

We were scrappy, tenacious, and annoyingly stubborn. We always found a way.

Plus, we had an ace up our sleeve with Fen. She might be able to provide information we hadn't had before.

"What about Fen?" I asked.

He looked at me, a bit puzzled, "What about her?"

"What if she can help us fix the ship?"

He thought about it for a few minutes and nodded.

"It makes sense, but I'm not sure how she would be able to help. Aside from making me look inept in a fight and talking into your brain, I don't see what her abilities would be."

"That's because you're only looking at her physically and automatically judging. What if she's smarter than we realize?"

We spent the rest of the night talking. His lips moved, and there were moments when words didn't even come out of them.

Over the next two days, I was back in the infirmary. The teams Rouhr had sent out to Einhiv had returned with survivors.

The news was terrible. Einhiv had been overwhelmed by people changing.

The clinic had been full, and despite the teams' best efforts, they hadn't convinced everyone to leave. Many people had decided to stay to be with their family, to help, or because they didn't trust these new people.

The teams had come back with only a small handful of people, just under twenty in total.

I went about checking them, searching for any signs of infection. None of them were. I breathed a sigh of relief, as this meant that at least these people wouldn't be used against us.

The memory of my own fight with the Queen and what I knew of the hybridism so far terrified me still.

To know that I was useless in stopping it as long as there was no cure pissed me off, too. I didn't like the idea of being useless...or lost when it came to a treatment.

Even the idea that the equipment here was better than what I had at Einhiv didn't make me feel better.

I was happy to see Tona and Skit. They had made an impression on the team leaders and were talking with Vrehx and Tu'ver at the far end of the infirmary.

"Excuse me, gentlemen, mind if I interrupt?" I asked as I walked over.

Tona and Skit both smiled and nodded when they saw me.

"Of course." Vrehx turned to the two. "As soon as she's finished with you, come see me in the hangar bay. I think we all have information to share with one another."

The guards nodded and Vrehx left. I asked how they were, and they were quiet as they told me that they were fine. They were blunt with their answers, and when I was finally able to get them to speak more than one-syllable words, they told me that none of the other guards had made it.

The hybrids had made the guards their focus in their attacks. They then explained that the "attacks" were not meant to kill, but to infect.

When the teams said that they were friends with me

and Sakev, they had hesitated in joining them because they felt slightly betrayed that we hadn't been truthful with them. It was the fact that everything Sakev had told them had been honest and true, and worked, that swayed them. Skit told me that Vrehx had turned off his own disguise belt, to show who they were, and when the others followed suit, they agreed to come with.

After a long day of checking everyone out and refitting the infirmary to handle humans as well as the other four hundred races aboard this damn thing, I went and found Sakev and talked to him. He had seen Tona and Skit, and while they had been a bit cold to him, they did acknowledge him and thanked him.

He gave me a kiss and sent me on my way as he told me he still had some things to finish. I went to our room and sat down to think.

Did we have an ace to play with Fen? Was she useful to us, or could she be?

Could the other humans put aside their species-phobia enough to work with us? How would we win this fight that had been accidentally brought to our world?

Then I wondered what life would be like amongst the stars.

EVIE

Despite the heat and humidity, the strange being's hands were cool and smooth. Not like the hands of the Xathi Queen, who could've passed for an ice carving, but more like a river rock.

You don't have to make those odd gestures when you speak to me. Her eyes went wide, which was saying something since they were already twice the size of a normal human eye. *Unless you must make those gestures when you speak. I don't mean to cause offense.*

I laughed out loud. Sakev, who was walking a few paces in front of us, looked over his shoulder.

"What?" He was trying to look suspicious, but I think he was just feeling left out.

"I'll tell you later." I winked. "We're having girl talk."

"That sounds horrifying." He shuddered and faced

forward once more.

I gave the lithe being a nod, and she placed her hand on my temple once more.

I can hear your thoughts just as you can hear mine. Our minds speak the same language, though our tongues do not.

Oh, then it's definitely not necessary for me to make those odd gestures.

It was difficult to keep my eyes open while she spoke to me. It was like my entire being was being pulled into my consciousness. I felt her other arm resting between my shoulders, guiding me as we walked.

Do you have a name?

Of sorts. Her voice was deep and lyrical. *You may call me Fen.*

I'm Evie. The angry red guy is Sakev. I felt something like laugh reverberate through her consciousness. *What are you? If you don't mind me asking.*

I am a Urai.

I'd never heard of Urai. Then again, I hadn't heard of Skotans, K'ver, or Valorni until they dropped from the sky. Eventually, I would get used to the idea that the universe was infinitely larger than my human mind could grasp, but today was not that day.

Do you know what we are?

You are a human. He is a Skotan. My people have come across Skotans before, but never humans. Your kind seemed so small and safe in your little corner of the galaxy. There was a quality to her voice and the way she formed her thoughts that made her seem ancient.

But you knew of us?

Yes. If one of us knows of you, we all know of you.

My eyes flew open, and I recoiled. The Urai must've been a hive-minded species. After my encounters with the hybrids and the Xathi, I was wary.

Sakev heard my quick movements and immediately spun around, blaster at the ready. Fen raised her hands and bowed her head as a gesture of submissive peace.

"Her name's Fen," I said to Sakev.

I wasn't sure if I wanted to tell him that she was part of a hive mind. Knowing the Xathi the way he did, I wouldn't blame him if he shot her, but Fen hadn't done anything to harm me. If she did, I knew Sakev would be on it.

Fen offered me her hands. A silent request.

I nodded.

She placed her hand against my temple once more.

Your mind has been exposed before, hasn't it?

I nodded.

Yes, it feels familiar. Your mind hosted a Xathi Queen. Only someone with great strength of mind and heart can repel a Xathi Queen.

You know about the Xathi? I asked. *Can you help us fight them?*

Perhaps. But I ask you to hear my story first. When I am finished, you and your companion can decide for yourselves if you want my aid.

"She knows things about the Xathi," I said out loud to Sakev.

"Can she help us?" Sakev lowered his blaster but didn't put it away.

"She wants to help. She said she's going to tell me her story, then we can decide if we want her help."

"Sounds suspicious." Sakev narrowed his eyes.

"It sounds honest to me." I shrugged. "Please, Sakev? Let's give her a chance. She might know something that could really help us."

"I can't say no to you." A smile broke through Sakev's serious demeanor. "Let's walk and talk, though. Or, well, I guess not talk. Walk and...communicate telepathically."

I nodded for Fen to resume her story. We stepped carefully through the underbrush to avoid breaking contact.

My people, the Urai, are one of the oldest species in the vast expanse of space. We pride ourselves on being intergalactic peacekeepers. We were confined to a single home world once, but we outlived it, just as you humans have outlived your Earth. Rather than find a new planet, we decided to make our lives in the stars.

Okay, this didn't sound too bad so far.

But it wasn't just a worn-out planet that influenced our decision to perpetually travel. Yes, we are a hive-minded species, but we do possess some level of individual autonomy. And like all species, we have our good, and we have our bad.

A faction of our people believed themselves to be superior over all other lifeforms. They enslaved a lesser species and genetically enhanced them, so they could be better workers.

When that wasn't satisfactory, some of the Urai took control of the minds of the lesser species. We are not naturally gifted with mind-controlling abilities, though we communicate telepathically. The process was experimental and ultimately disastrous. The minds of the lesser species were fractured beyond repair. We should have killed them all, but we didn't. We exiled them into the darkest reaches of space.

I knew where this was going.

Those exiled creatures became the Xathi you are fighting against today. After realizing the horror we'd unleashed upon the galaxy, my people set out to right their wrong.

But the Xathi had developed their own hive-mind that was more synchronized than ours. They think as one being. It's difficult to defeat an enemy with a million arms and eyes. We were unsuccessful in our attempt to wipe them out. We have tried to make amends by offering our aid when the Xathi attack a new world.

I was silent for a long while. It was a considerable amount of information to take in. I wanted to tell

Sakev, but I didn't know how to put everything into words.

Is that why you were on the Aurora? I asked. I needed to know the rest.

Yes. We were unable to prevent a Xathi attack, so we decided to help the survivors. We joined up with a resistance group who'd learned of the Xathi. Several species from all over the quadrant banded together. In fact, I believe they were traveling to Sakev's home world. Somehow, the Xathi were able to intercept us. They stole the minds of the Aurora passengers and left the ship to drift through space. It was luck that we fell through the rift.

Perhaps that was something Sakev ought to know. Fen and her people had been trying to reach his home world.

Sakev was part of the team that first traveled to the Aurora. They didn't find any survivors. How did you survive the fall through the rift? I asked.

I'd heard about the *Aurora* from Vidia. She'd told me the rescue team ran countless tests and scans but found nothing except for some eerie surveillance footage and audio clips. I assumed the audio clips were left by the other species sharing the *Aurora*.

I was in stasis, along with a handful of other Urai. Jumping constantly between galaxies is taxing on the body. Those of us who were in stasis were the only survivors.

What a rude awakening!

The Xathi attacked Fraga in the dead of night. I'd been sleeping soundly on a pull-out couch in my office after working late when chaos exploded. I suspected Fen must've felt something similar.

How many Urai survived? I asked. I felt a wave of pain crash through her mind.

Ten. Out of hundreds that were aboard the Aurora. Thousands, including the other races.

I felt her grief as if it were my own.

I'm so sorry for your loss. May I tell Sakev what you've told me?

Fen nodded and retracted her hand from my temple. My eyes fluttered open.

"I wish you could see how strange the pair of you look," Sakev said when he realized my eyes were open.

"It's a good thing no one important is around to see us," I quipped. "Now hush. I've something important to tell you."

I relayed everything Fen told me, including as many details as I could remember. Though Fen's people were responsible for the creation of the Xathi, I didn't believe she was an enemy. I needed Sakev to see what a powerful ally she and the other Urai could be.

"That's insane. You realize how insane that is, right?" Sakev demanded when I was finished.

Fen watched us with patient eyes.

"How is it any more insane than anything else that's

happened since that damn rift opened?" I argued. "Don't you think General Rouhr should see her? He'd want to know everything she knows!"

"Evie—"

"I'm going to keep arguing until you agree. You may as well spare yourself the headache."

Sakev rubbed his face and sighed. His shoulders sagged in defeat.

"Fine," he relented. "But tell her she hasn't earned my trust yet."

Sakev doesn't trust you, but I do. I persuaded Sakev to take you to his General, I explained to Fen.

Fen seemed pleased.

Excellent. I am eager to learn what he has planned. Do you know if he's doing anything about the rift?

I wouldn't know. But our main focus thus far has been the Xathi.

I often forgot about the rift. I spent little time outside and was more concerned with what was happening on the ground.

It's imperative that the rift is closed at once, Fen insisted. *A rift of that size left open for too long can rip a planet apart.*

"Oh, shit!" I exclaimed.

"What now?" Sakev sounded exhausted.

"Double time, Sakev!" I marched on, overtaking him. Fen was right on my heels. "We've got a planet to save."

"Didn't we always?"

EPILOGUE

Evie

I sat, cross-legged, on the bed in my new room. Now that all the people rescued from Einhiv had been given a clean bill of health, General Rouhr had insisted I take a few days off. I wasn't complaining. There were loads of medical journals I'd been dying to read. Apparently, Tu'ver had made some adjustments to the onboard library and greatly expanded the collection.

"You can't possibly still be reading?" The door to the cabin slid open, and Sakev entered, carrying three trays overloaded with food from the mess hall. "Seriously, have you even moved since I left this morning?"

"I rolled over once." I set my datapad on the nightstand and hurried to help Sakev before he dropped anything. Most of the food was unrecognizable to me, though the cook had been incorporating more human recipes into his menu.

"One of the perks of constantly getting kitchen duty." Sakev retrieved two plates from one of the cabinets, though we never ended up using them. "Good ol' Snipes is happy to let me take as much food as I want."

There were certainly a lot of meat dishes. I decided it was best if I didn't know exactly what they were.

Sakev and I sat across from each other with our bounty spread out between us. I immediately went for the noodles. They were my weakness.

"Will I like that?" I asked, jabbing my fork at pieces of meat covered in an orange sauce.

"Probably not." Sakev replied before taking a big bite for himself.

"Are you just saying that because you want it all to yourself?" I lifted an eyebrow.

"Yes," Sakev admitted. I laughed, almost choking on a roasted veggie.

"That's okay, you can have it." I took a forkful of meat with a slightly blue tinge to it. Surprisingly delicious.

"You're being awfully sweet this evening." Sakev leaned over the sprawl of food to peck my cheek. He left a smear of sauce on my face, which I immediately wiped away, feigning disgust. "What's the occasion?"

"I had a great idea today. I'm excited to start working on it tomorrow."

"What's that?"

"I found one of the pod scanners I used back at the Einhiv clinic. It must have been in my pocket when you carried me out," I began. "I was thinking we could take that concept but incorporate the med bay's ability to detect hybridism."

"'We?'" Sakev asked.

"I'll need your help, of course!" I could see the excitement building in his eyes. "It's not like I can make them. You're the one who's good with your hands."

"I can show you how good they are, in case you forgot." Sakev winked. I gave his shoulder a small, playful shove.

"How could I ever?" I batted my lashes. "But, seriously, what do you think of my idea?"

"I think it's fantastic." His genuine smile made my heart skip a beat. "If you let me tinker around with the pod scanner, I can probably figure something out."

"That would be great!" I beamed. "I was thinking we could make enough so that the teams could carry them on patrols. If they found any people, they could give them a quick scan to make sure they're clean."

"That would make patrols seem less stupid," Sakev agreed.

"And if the scans were detailed enough, I could learn more about hybridism," I went on. I was on a roll now. Poor Sakev was just going to have to ride it out. "And guess what else?"

"What?" His smile was indulgent.

"I talked to Vidia. She wants me and Jeneva to lead a seminar for humans about fighting off mental influences. I'm sure the crew would be allowed to take part, too. I can ask General Rouhr tomorrow." I paused.

Sakev was looking at me with a strange, sleepy smile.

"What?" I asked, suddenly self-conscious.

"Nothing," Sakev said. "You're just as adorable as you are brilliant." A blush quickly heated my cheeks. I took a quick bite of something spicy to hide it.

"I'm an asshole," Sakev said suddenly.

"The first step is admitting it." I gave him an encouraging pat on the shoulder before diving in for another bite of another mystery meat.

"Very funny." Sakev rolled his eyes. "Will you let me finish?"

"Go ahead." I bowed my head.

"I'm an asshole. I'm not the best at being serious. One of my jokes is probably going to get me killed one day. But you mean the world to me, Evie. I know I have a weird way of showing it sometimes. But I need you to know that I'd do anything for you. I love you, Evie."

I was speechless, completely stunned. I knew Sakev cared. True, he was terrible at verbalizing those sorts of things, but I still knew. Just as he, hopefully, knew I cared deeply for him.

"Evie." His voice was achingly gentle as he brushed a finger across my cheek. "Why are you crying?"

Embarrassed, I quickly wiped at my face. I hadn't realized I was.

"I don't know," I laughed, realizing I looked completely ridiculous. "I'm happy! Sakev, you've saved my life countless times. The memory of you brought me back from life as a mindless slave. You piss me off more than anyone else I know, but I love it. I love everything about you. I love you, Sakev."

He kissed me over our makeshift buffet. I didn't even care that he was probably spilling sauce all over the bedsheets. He hugged me tightly, but only with one arm. I could feel his shoulder moving.

"Sakev, what are you doing?" I asked.

"You were eating all the sautéed marsh root!" he said defensively, before sneaking in a mouthful. Laughing, I pushed him back to his side of the buffet. There was the Sakev I knew and loved.

"I literally had one bite!" I said in defense. "And it was disgusting."

Sakev looked at me, mouth agape.

"You take that back!" he warned.

"Why? If I think it's gross, then you get to eat all of it," I pointed out. Sakev paused and considered my statement.

"Never mind. Carry on," he decreed. After polishing off the marsh root, he looked up at me. "We should go back to that cabin for a little getaway."

"That'd be nice," I admitted. "Maybe after we finish the new pod scanners."

"Maybe. I was thinking we'd go sooner than that," Sakev suggested. "Before things start changing. It's times like this that make it easy to forget we're at war. I just want to enjoy as many moments like this as I can while there's still time."

I understood what he was trying to say. There were some tough choices ahead. Not just for Sakev and me, but for everyone aboard the *Vengeance*. But I didn't want to dwell on that right now. That kind of thinking had kept me awake at night. I wasn't about to let it ruin this time with Sakev.

"If I've learned anything since I met you, it's that you and I are damn good at finding a way out of messes. I don't think this will be any different," I said with confidence.

"Oh, yeah?" Sakev challenged. "What makes you so sure?"

"The sky of my world broke apart. Everything I thought I knew to be true changed. There were times I was so sure I was going to die I thought my heart would quit on me right then and there. But I survived. You survived. All of the horrible things that happened are what brought me to you. Now that I have you, I'm determined to keep going."

"That was cheesed," Sakev laughed.

"The word is *cheesy*, you big oaf," I giggled.

We didn't talk about the war, the Xathi, or anything else unpleasant that night. We ate our food, made each other laugh, and kept each other close as we waited for the sky to fall again.

This time…we'd wait for it together.

I love Sakev... but I think I'd understand if Evie occasionally wanted to smother him with a pillow....

They'll always tease each other, but you know they'll always have each others backs, and that's one of the things I love about them.

Next up?

You'd be a bit of a b*tch, too.

If everyone has left you, died on you, and laughed at your dreams, you might have a few issues. And then to have your planet invaded right when you're about to follow through on the one thing you have left?

Done.

Amira's not particularly interested in making friends. When she hears a rumor that the alien war ship may soon depart, she's done. This time she'll be the one doing the leaving.

But no matter how hard she makes her heart, she can't help but want to help the refugees sheltering in the *Vengeance.*

And when a certain green skinned alien makes her a proposal, it's only for the other humans she's considering it.

Right?

Daxion is used to being the big-brother of the team. The oldest of ten, he'd learned to roll with almost anything long before he joined the alliance against the Xathi.

Tiny, prickly Amira spikes his curiosity, and his desire. He's determined to keep her safe .

What he's feeling is anything but brotherly. He has a new mission now: work his way past the barriers around her heart.

But with the war against the Xathi taking a new turn, will they have a chance?

Coming in January! Available for pre-order now!

XOXO,

Elin

Daxion
It was my turn for night patrol inside the ship. I didn't mind, it gave me time to think about my family back home and wonder if they were still safe.

As the oldest of ten, it was my responsibility to look out for my siblings. When I joined the military, it was with their protection in mind.

Here, cut off from the rest of the war, I'd heard nothing. I could only hope.

The night shift went about their normal business on the second level, constantly maintaining the ship, trying to conduct repairs, and working alongside the humans.

Sakev's friends, Tona and Skit, were particularly enthusiastic about learning the ship's systems and proving their worth. I admired their tenacity to prove themselves, especially since Skit was so tiny compared to the rest of us.

Level three checked out. I double-checked all the doors that were supposed to be locked and verified everything was how it should be on level three. My teammates felt that this was extremely boring work, but that didn't matter.

It needed to be done.

The sweep of level four's living quarters showed nothing unusual, so back down to the main level with the refugee bay, infirmary, hangar bay, and several storage bays.

Where the sight of someone trying to hide behind a crate drew my attention.

I followed quietly, something that even Tu'ver would have found miraculous, considering my size. I couldn't tell if it was a man or a woman, but whoever it was, they were skinny and carrying a pack.

The form flitted from crate to crate, making its way towards the ship's exit door.

That was something I couldn't allow, not without General Rouhr's prior approval.

From behind a support pillar, I finally realized our potential runaway was a human woman.

Perhaps a less confrontational approach would be better.

As she neared the door, I stepped out from behind

the pillar and blocked the door, my arms folded across my chest.

I smiled down at her, but she still let out a small yelp.

"Good evening. Is there something that I might be able to help you with, Miss...?" I let the syllable hang with the idea that she would fill in her name.

She looked familiar, but I hadn't spent enough time around the refugees to easily tell them apart.

She looked up at me, anger a quick flash on her face as she dialed up a look of innocence, "Is there a problem?"

"I must apologize, but I can't let you leave the ship. It's far too dangerous to go out at night alone, Miss..." I tried to bait her, again, into giving me her name. She was so familiar...

She didn't bite. "You can't keep me here," she started, her voice obviously forced to be calm and level. "I'm not a prisoner. I have the right to leave anytime I want."

I nodded, "And I agree with you, Miss..."

She huffed a bit, "My name is Amira."

Of course. Jeneva's sister.

I nodded again, "And I am Daxion, of the first strike team. As I was saying, Miss Amira, I agree with you. You truly are not a prisoner, and you do have the ability to leave the ship, but I really must recommend you not leave at night...or alone."

She tried to say something, but I held up my hands to forestall her. "The situation is far too dangerous around here at night. I know that you've grown up on this world and know its creatures, but the Xathi are much different than anything else out there. They don't need light to find you. Please, for your own safety, stay on board."

"Are you really not hearing me right now? You can't keep me here. If I want to leave, I can leave," she insisted.

I decided to change tactics a bit. "If I may ask, why are you so insistent on leaving?"

She looked around and shuffled from foot to foot, then glared at me. "You're leaving anyway. Why should I stay?"

"Leave? What makes you believe that we will leave?"

With an exasperated sigh that seemed to indicate she was already tired of me and my questions, she snapped, "I heard your general plans to leave and close the rift, leaving Ankau to deal with the Xathi on our own. Someone even said you'd take us with you and leave the rest of the humans. How is that any better?"

I tried to steer her away from the door, but she resisted. I relented, but took a step back to better block the door. "There have been no official decisions made, it was only a possibility."

"It's still a possibility of you people running away

and leaving us to deal with those bugs. I will not leave my home," she said.

"If we were to leave, it would not be before giving the people of the planet the tools and knowledge needed to fight the Xathi or taking you with us."

I hesitated a second as I looked at her. If rumors were flying about the general's plans, it wouldn't hurt to try to set things straight. "To be honest, even if we decided to leave, General Rouhr would not do so without careful consideration. Additionally, the *Vengeance* still needs major repairs. Those will take a significant amount of time. We aren't going anywhere. We aren't leaving you."

That was reassuring, right?

Apparently not.

"It doesn't matter what you try to tell me, you're still thinking about leaving us to those monsters. The people deserve to know what's happening."

"Shouldn't you have all the information before you run off to tell people half of a story?"

That stopped her. She looked at me with a look that I interpreted as resignation.

I had won that point, I just hadn't known we were playing a game.

She tapped her foot on the deck and bit her lip in frustration, then decided to argue her point again. "You still can't keep me here. I have every right to leave."

"That you do," I said with a nod, "and I don't deny it. However, I would prefer not to arrest you."

She looked at me, bewilderment on her face and in her eyes. "What do you mean? Why would you arrest me?"

I pointed to the pack in her hand. "If you try to leave with those things, that would be considered theft. I would be forced to detain you and place you in the brig." I tried my best to hide my smile.

"You...you...how...why...but..." she stammered as she tried to find words.

"Inside that pack," I pointed at the pack on her shoulder, "I'm guessing you have some rations and a blaster. If you were smart, and I'm guessing you are, you also have a heat sensor in that pack, so you can see what's out there in the dark. Am I right?"

I folded my arms over my chest again.

She just nodded.

I didn't bother to hide my smile this time.

"Miss Amira, if you promise to go back to your room, at least for the night, and hand over the pack, I won't officially report this incident."

"Why not?" she asked, eyes narrowed.

"Because, you should be allowed to make your own decisions." She started to say something, but I kept talking, "If you wish to leave in the morning, I won't stop you."

After a few moments, she relented, handed over the pack, and stomped out of the hangar bay, presumably back to her room.

The final point went to me.

Right?

I watched her go. She wasn't the type to give up so easily.

How long would my victory last in the game I hadn't realized we were playing?

AMIRA

I woke to someone touching my shoulder.

Not yet awake, I rolled to the opposite side of my bed as fast as I could, almost falling off the bed completely. I grabbed for anything within reach, ready to use it as weapon, then the lights turned on.

"Jeneva!" I lowered the datapad I'd been reading late into the night and set it back down gently, as if to hide the fact that I'd been going to hurl it at my sister's head. To be fair, I didn't know it was my sister at the time.

"I thought waking you gently was a smart plan." Jeneva tried to smile. "I guess it backfired."

"Why are you waking me up in the first place?" I snapped. I closed my eyes and took a breath. I'd promised Jeneva I would work on my temper.

Not that she was keeping up with any of her promises.

This was the first time I'd seen her in a week, maybe longer. It was difficult to keep track of the days on the ship. There weren't a lot of windows, and even though the ship's lights dimmed for the night cycle, it didn't seem to make a difference in my brain.

"It's nearly midday." Jeneva blinked in surprise.

I was a late sleeper, it was true. After last night's misadventure, it was hours after midnight before I got back to my room.

"I waited in the refugee bay for hours, but you never showed up. I figured you were here."

"So, you just came in?" I asked. "Wait, how did you get in?"

"You never changed the code from when this was my room," Jeneva explained.

Jeneva now bunked with one of the strike team leaders, a Skotan named Vrehx. From what I could tell, he was great at what he did around the ship. Jeneva seemed happy too, happier than I ever remember her being.

The memories left a bitter taste in my mouth. When we were kids, I always remember Jeneva being unhappy or uncomfortable. No one in our family realized it at the time, but Jeneva could sense other people's feelings and moods.

When she was a kid, she couldn't control it. She was often in a great amount of pain, especially after our parents died, so she picked up and moved to the middle of the forest for over a decade. She left with no explanation and hardly a goodbye.

It wasn't until we were reunited on the *Vengeance* that I learned all of this.

"That doesn't give you the right to come and go as you please," I sniffed.

I'd been so angry at Jeneva for so long. If I'm being honest, I'm still angry. After I almost lost Jeneva for a second time, permanently, I swore I would try to build our relationship into what it was always supposed to be.

Which was harder than I'd hoped.

"And you don't have the right to sneak off the ship, the only safe place for miles, in the middle of the night," Jeneva shot back.

Now I knew why she was here.

"Did your boyfriend report me?" I glared.

Jeneva gave me a stern look. "No, Dax came to talk to me privately. Vrehx doesn't even know. I can't believe you would do something so risky and stupid!"

I wondered if Jeneva could feel what I was feeling now. "He had no right to go to you."

I couldn't think of anything else to say. Last night was not a shining moment of genius for me, but that didn't mean that Valorni could go around telling everyone.

It wasn't his business anyway, he'd done his job.

He kept me from doing something dangerous and stopped me from technically stealing, which I felt guilty about. There was no need for him to get involved any further.

"He's concerned for your safety," Jeneva argued.

"Well, that makes one person," I muttered.

"Excuse me?" Jeneva's eyes narrowed.

"Maybe if I had someone to talk to, like a *sister*, I wouldn't have tried to go through with such a stupid plan!" I exclaimed.

"You can always talk to me." Jeneva looked hurt.

"Only if I can find you. This ship is huge, Jeneva. I don't even know where you do your work. I never know when you go out into the field. I wouldn't know if something happened to you!"

"Of course, you would know." Jeneva spoke in a soft, gentle voice, as if I were a child. "Just like how I would know if something happened to you."

"Last week, I got sick and had to spend the night in the med bay with Dr. Parr." I folded my arms across my chest.

It wasn't anything serious. I just ate some alien food from the mess hall that I didn't know I was allergic to.

"Oh." Jeneva looked down at her feet. "Are you okay?"

"No, I died." I rolled my eyes.

"That isn't helping, Amira."

"What's not helping is you coming into my room in an attempt to be the sister you never were!" Tears welled in my eyes, and I looked away before Jeneva could see them.

I wanted this to be better.

I wanted **me** to be better.

I really did. But it was so hard to get out of my head, out of the past.

"I actually believed you were serious when you said you wanted to be more involved in my life. I guess that stopped when you met your alien soulmate."

I reacted badly the first day I was brought to the *Vengeance.* Jeneva had gone out of her way to rescue me and quite a few others. I was in shock, scared and surrounded by aliens and my long-lost sister.

I snapped. I yelled. I was mean.

It had earned me the title of "Jeneva's ungrateful little sister". I'd been able to drop that title since, but it still bothered me. Jeneva abandoned me for years, right after our parents died, but I'm the one who had to do all the work to fix our relationship because I'd had one bad day?

I'd done everything I could for people in the refugee

bay. I helped Dr. Parr when she had her hands full. I helped Vidia teach lessons to the kids.

I even learned how to knit, so I could make blankets, hats, and socks! It was bitterly cold on the ship sometimes.

But it was never enough to make Jeneva pick me over Vrehx.

"I don't know what to do," Jeneva said so quietly, I could barely hear her. "You're angry with me when we don't spend time together, but when we do spend time together, you push me away. I don't know how to win."

"I get angry when you tell me you want things to be better and then don't follow through," I explained. "I push you away because I don't like feeling that you think you can show up whenever you want and expect things to be perfect."

"For the first time in a very long time, I have a real life. I can be around people and not feel like my head is going to explode. Can you understand that?" Jeneva pleaded.

"I can understand that it must have been horrible dealing with that growing up. I can understand how you thought the only solution was to live far away from people. But I don't understand why you shut me out of your life for ten years."

I didn't expect this. I wasn't prepared for this

conversation. We hadn't talked about any of it since we were reunited.

"I couldn't bear to face you." Tears slipped down her cheeks. "I'd caused you so much pain."

"Did it ever occur to you that I would've been in much less pain if you'd just talked to me?" I pressed. "No, rather than own up to the damage you did, you decided to hide. That was a choice you made. I'd be able to forgive that, forgive *everything*, if you'd stop pretending that a few civilized conversations and a joke here and there are enough to fix what's broken."

"It's better than nothing." Jeneva didn't sound convinced by her own words. "I want to be the sister I should have been. I just don't know how." Understatement of the year.

"I'm not trying to hurt you, but the bottom line is that I don't trust you. It's hard for me to trust people. It takes time."

I didn't want to say it was her fault that I had trust issues. It might be true, but she was already hurting. I didn't need to make it worse.

"I understand," Jeneva nodded.

"I think it's best if you leave now. This was a lot. I think we both need some time."

I didn't want her to see how shaken I was. I was a minute away from a complete breakdown. I didn't like anyone seeing me in that state.

"Okay." Her voice was weak with defeat as she slowly left the room. She paused at the doorway. "We'll talk later, okay?"

"Okay," I replied. I doubted that she would reach out to me later.

The door slid shut. I sat down on the bed, my legs shaking. My breathing was ragged as my throat felt tighter. I buried my face in my pillow and screamed.

After my parents died, I refused to let myself be swept away by grief. I had to keep pushing, so my life wouldn't fall apart.

I came up with a system for dealing with my emotions: The Five-Minute System. What the name lacked in creativity, it made up for in efficiency.

I set a timer for five minutes. In that five minutes, I could do whatever I needed to do: cry, scream, break something, whatever. But when the five minutes were up, I had to get it together.

I pulled up the timer on the mounted clock and started the countdown. I think I'd subconsciously trained myself to respond to the timer. Not even two seconds had passed, and I was on the deck, hugging my pillow and sobbing.

I refrained from breaking anything. Nothing here actually belonged to me. When the timer was up, I calmed my shuddering breaths, washed my face, and started the day.

I needed to get out of that damn room.

DAXION

General Rouhr called all members of each strike team to his conference room for a meeting.

I arrived first, followed by Tu'ver, Vrehx, and eventually all the others, including Engineer Thribb. Axtin and Sakev were the last ones to arrive, laughing as they entered the room.

Rouhr started as they took their seats. "We have some serious things we need to talk about, and I want to start with the biggest issue on our plate." He paused, but I knew what he was going to say. We all did.

"The Xathi."

Since Sakev's return from Einhiv, there had been only one conversation swirling through the crew, apparently even bleeding over into the gossip of the refugees, judging by last night's interaction with Amira.

Should we find a way off the planet or continue to fight?

"We need to decide if we are going to stay on Ankau and continue to fight the Xathi, or if we're going to take the information we have already and try to get off-world," Rouhr said, echoing my thoughts.

Axtin was the first to respond. "Are we even able to leave? The *Vengeance* is still partially buried, and there aren't enough materials to fix her properly, even if we had everyone in Duvest working to get us the parts."

Thribb responded. "You are very correct, Axtin. The ship is in a very awkward predicament at the moment, as are we."

Thribb got up from his seat and walked over to the main screen. He brought up an inventory list and continued, "Our current situation does not afford us much opportunity for repairs. If we could conduct repairs without interruption, I estimate that it would take us just under a year to make the proper repairs needed for sustained space travel."

"How long just to get her in the air?" Axtin asked.

Thribb nodded at Axtin. "That would still take us several weeks, if we were uninterrupted. However, with the Xathi threat and the constant need for defense and patrols, we will need several months in order to get the *Vengeance* flying again."

"Then what is the point in trying to figure out if we should stay or not?" Karzin asked. "Seems to me, our circumstances have already decided for us."

I had to agree with him to a degree. If the ship would be that difficult to repair, then all our efforts should be on stopping the Xathi.

However, there was something he had missed, and I wasn't the only one who saw it.

Takar spoke up. "Except we have a problem with

our supplies, Karzin." He looked at his team leader. "We don't have the munitions needed to maintain a prolonged battle with the Xathi. Even if we were able to get weapons from the humans who are on our side, our own supplies are running low."

"What about those grenades Axtin and his human managed to create in Duvest?" Rokul, Takar's brother, asked.

Takar turned to look at his brother. "They are useful, but not fool-proof. Also, their range is limited, and their efficiency is dependent upon how many Xathi are in the immediate area."

Rouhr spoke up, taking control of the conversation. "Takar makes a valid point. We are limited with our supplies, and with more humans coming to stay every week, our stores are being taxed more than expected. We need to choose which direction is best for us. I see four possibilities, and one of them is not even a choice."

As he spoke, I agreed. Four options, none fabulous.

Choice one, we could continue to fight the Xathi and try to figure out what they were up to.

Choice two, we could concentrate our efforts on repairing the ship and leaving.

Choice three, we could split our concentration between ship repair and fighting, which is what we had been doing, with limited effectiveness.

Choice four? We could decide that we no longer

stood a chance and conduct a final assault where we would most likely be destroyed.

"Sir?" Everyone turned their attention to me. I rarely ever spoke during meetings unless addressed first.

I didn't need to add extra words to the briefings. Usually things were pretty clear-cut.

But not anymore.

"What are we looking for exactly in regard to the Xathi?"

"May I?" Vrehx asked Rouhr.

Rouhr nodded and Vrehx got to his feet. He always talked better when he walked around.

"The Xathi are not acting as they normally do. When they attacked each of our planets, their method was to simply attack, destroy, and drain as many resources as possible, correct?"

Everyone in the room nodded in agreement.

It was how the Xathi had always worked. They would swoop in, cause devastation, and while the Soldiers were fighting the planet's defenders, the Xathi Workers and Harvesters would denude the planet of whatever resources they could get.

It had happened on each of our homeworlds.

It wasn't something any of us would ever forget.

"They're not doing that here," Vrehx continued. "They've changed direction since we first landed, started an entirely new operation, as far as we can tell. They're working on creating the hybrids, taking over the human population."

He paused, scowling. "My original thought was they were using the humans to repair their own ship, but our patrols indicate that that's not happening, at least as far as we can see. The holes we blew in it," he said with a nod to Axtin, "are still there. They're using the humans for something else."

General Rouhr took the conversation back from Vrehx. "That is why we need to figure out what they're up to. This is a complete flip from what they normally do, and it has me concerned."

Thribb spoke up again, his distaste at his own words showing. "Sir," he said with a hint of respect in his voice, "I humbly disagree. As stated earlier, we are running low on munitions and other supplies. And despite the admirable showings of the humans that are working with us, we are limited in skilled warriors. I can't believe that I'm about to say this," and he shook his head as he did, "but I believe we should concentrate on fixing the ship and leaving this planet. It is better to live so we can fight again than to throw away our lives and never fight again."

It was an old Valorni saying, but every species I'd ever met had a variant of it.

Didn't mean I liked it.

"If the Xathi are acting differently, there must be a reason, and we need to know what that reason is. It could be the answer to defeating them," Takar argued.

Tu'ver nodded in agreement. "There is a chance that the humans either know something or are in possession of something that the Xathi want. That could be beneficial for us if we found it first."

Engineer Thribb spoke up. "That is a very logical argument, Tu'ver. However, our current limited supplies do not afford us an opportunity to conduct such an investigation. Our best course of action is to repair the ship as best as possible, then make our way off the planet and back through the rift."

Rouhr stood, silencing the rest of us. "Let me pose this question to everyone. If we were to leave the planet and escape through the rift, how would your consciences handle the idea of abandoning the humans here? Humans whom we have become friends with, might I remind you."

The room was quiet. Each team had their own human contacts around the continent and had made friends with several of the humans on board. Tona and Skit, as well as other guards and soldiers, had already made an impression on each team, as had the women who had become part of our crew's families.

Evie was invaluable in the infirmary and in her study of the hybrids. Jeneva had taught each of us how to survive the wilderness where even the trees tried to kill you. Mariella and Leena worked in the lab, finding new ways to deal with the Xathi and how to modify the neuro-weapons we had invented.

Rouhr broke the silence. "I, in good conscience, cannot fathom the idea of leaving behind so many people to try to defend themselves against an enemy that even we, with superior technology, struggle with. Even if it is the logical decision," he said with a nod to Thribb, "I believe that it is the wrong decision. But... that is my belief. Each of you have laid out your thoughts, at least most of you have, and you all make compelling cases. We just need to figure out our plan of action. We can't split our concentrations anymore. It's holding us back and hurting us. We need to choose."

I already knew my choice. I wanted to know why the Xathi were behaving as they were. If there was something in the human mind, or whatever, that could benefit all of us, I wanted to know what it was.

Then, something occurred to me. "Sir? What about the *Aurora*?"

Rouhr looked at me and smiled. "According to Fen's latest reports, the Xathi population in the Kangefi wetlands is negligible. She estimates single digits and believes it's because there are no humans left in the wetlands, so they've left the *Aurora* alone. Any that were there have either been infected or escaped. Actually, hold on."

The general looked down at his tablet, then smiled as he looked up. "Some good news, for a change. Fen and her people have agreed to share whatever resources they can spare."

A slight relaxing of tension rolled around the table. It meant that we had a little more to help keep ourselves going, no matter what decision we made.

At least for a little while.

He looked at Vrehx. "I need you and your team to go back to the *Aurora* and coordinate with Fen to run a proper inventory. Find out what kind of resources they have and what we can use."

"Aye, sir." Vrehx responded.

"Sir?" I asked.

"You're mighty talkative today, Dax." Rouhr smiled. "What is it?"

"I'd like to include Amira on this trip, if you wouldn't mind." It was a calculated gamble, but I had to ask.

"Why?"

"She's deeply embedded with the refugee population. We know how quickly rumors can fly when a crew is under tension. If the humans don't have information, they'll jump to conclusions. It's far too likely those conclusions could be an additional problem we'll need to attend to."

I shot a sly look towards my strike captain. "Besides, if Amira can participate and show her worth, that will make Jeneva happier, which will make Vrehx happier, which makes all of us happier. Sir."

From the corner of my eye, I could see Vrehx's scowl.

Rouhr grinned. "I understand. Very well, take her along."

This was going to be interesting.

GET DAXION NOW!

https://elinwynbooks.com/conquered-world-alien-romance/

PLEASE DON'T FORGET TO LEAVE A REVIEW!

Readers rely on your opinions, and your review can help others decide on what books they read. Make sure your opinion is heard and leave a review where you purchased this book!

Don't miss a new release! You can sign up for release alerts at both Amazon and Bookbub:

bookbub.com/authors/elin-wyn

amazon.com/author/elinwyn

For a free short story, opportunities for advance review copies, release news and the occasional cat picture, please join the newsletter!

https://elinwynbooks.com/newsletter-signup/

And don't forget the Facebook group, where I post sneak peeks of chapters and covers!

https://www.facebook.com/groups/ElinWyn/

DON'T MISS THE STAR BREED!

Given: Star Breed Book One

When a renegade thief and a genetically enhanced mercenary collide, space gets a whole lot hotter!

Thief Kara Shimsi has learned three lessons well - keep her head down, her fingers light, and her tithes to the syndicate paid on time.

But now a failed heist has earned her a death sentence - a one-way ticket to the toxic Waste outside the dome. Her only chance is a deal with the syndicate's most ruthless enforcer, a wolfish mountain of genetically-modified muscle named Davien.

The thought makes her body tingle with dread-or is it heat?

Mercenary Davien has one focus: do whatever is necessary to get the credits to get off this backwater mining colony and back into space. The last thing he wants is a smart-mouthed thief - even if she does have the clue he needs to hunt down whoever attacked the floating lab he and his created brothers called home.

Caring is a liability. Desire is a commodity. And love could get you killed.

https://elinwynbooks.com/star-breed/

ABOUT THE AUTHOR

I love old movies – *To Catch a Thief, Notorious, All About Eve* — and anything with Katherine Hepburn in it. Clever, elegant people doing clever, elegant things.

I'm a hopeless romantic.

And I love science fiction and the promise of space.

So it makes perfect sense to me to try to merge all of those loves into a new science fiction world, where dashing heroes and lovely ladies have adventures, get into trouble, and find their true love in the stars!

www.ingramcontent.com/pod-product-compliance
Lightning Source LLC
Chambersburg PA
CBHW070736180626
46818CB00007B/2869